# TED TAYLER

# GATHERING CLOUDS

BOOKS

# By Ted Tayler

## The Freeman Files

*Red Herring Season*

*Gathering Clouds*

*Still Standing*

Vinci Books

vinci-books.com

Published by Vinci Books Ltd in 2025

1

A CIP catalogue record for this book is available from the British Library.
Paperback ISBN: 9781036705091

# Chapter One

"WILL everything be ready for me to leave at eleven?" asked Gus.

"I don't see why not," said Grace. "My work is complete; we've all had long enough to get our contributions together."

"That's us told," said Neil quietly.

"What's the latest from the Met, guv?" asked Alex.

"DS Mercer tells me Rollins and Hatch have been questioned at length, plus several of their drivers," said Gus. "As you can imagine, the prime suspects didn't admit their guilt in the first five minutes. The Yeoh family statements shook Rollins's resolve somewhat when they were introduced into the equation. Given the intimidatory tactics Hatch and his cronies adopted, I don't think he believed any of his clients would ever have the guts to speak out. But, together with what we gathered from the Jade Garden's owners, the Met are confident of a positive result, even if it takes a while."

"Matt Archer was just in the wrong place at the wrong time, guv," said Blessing.

"None of us knows what's around the corner, Blessing," said Gus.

"I wonder what's next for us?" said Lydia.

"More of the same, I hope, Lydia," said Gus. "I hate surprises."

An hour later, Gus left the office to drive to London Road and his lunchtime meeting with Kenneth Truelove, the Chief Constable. Last week's clear-skied, icy weather had been replaced by a misty grey murk that seemed to last all day. Before you knew it, what little light there was had faded, and it was time to draw the curtains for another long night.

The outskirts of town were soon behind him, and there were no annoying holdups in Seend. Barely thirty minutes after leaving the Church Street car park, he arrived at the Wiltshire Police HQ on London Road. Gus began to wonder when he found a parking space not ten yards from the main building. He made his way slowly towards the front door.

"You look weary, Mr Freeman. Did you have a busy weekend?"

Gus looked up. It was Divya Yadav, the team's favourite Hub employee.

"Why are you always so cheerful, Divya?" he asked.

"I'm doing a job I love, married to a wonderful man who had his first weekend off in months. Life is good."

"My weekend was nothing special, Divya, unlike yours," said Gus. "I was in a good mood when I left the office, though, and I bear good tidings for the boss, but somehow I sense my day won't continue in the same vein. I smell trouble."

"There's been no announcement of any kind yet," said Divya, ensuring their conversation wasn't overheard. "But you must be psychic. I was only upstairs on the mezzanine for ten minutes, and it felt like everyone was holding their breath. Very odd. I can't imagine what it could be. There have been rumours, of course, but I tend to set them aside until I receive official confirmation."

"Rumours?" asked Gus.

"The PCC isn't halfway through his four-year stint yet, and in an article in the local newspaper on Friday, he stressed he was keen to leave his mark."

"Rather than the stain left by his predecessor," said Gus. "I can see his point. But, did he indicate how he might achieve this commendable aim for a legacy?"

"He was careful not to mention names, but he did sing the praises of an Assistant Chief Constable currently working in the Northeast."

"It's not news our Chief Constable's days are numbered," said Gus.

"Only the actual number of days remains to be determined, I suppose," said Divya. "No rest for the wicked. I must go."

Divya scurried across the car park towards the Hub building, and Gus went indoors. After briefly pausing at the Reception desk to sign in, he climbed the stairs and scanned the Administration area for friendly faces.

Kassie Trotter was on the far side of the office with her new trolley. She gave Gus a wave. Kenneth Truelove's door was closed, and there was no sign of Geoff Mercer yet. Thanks to his unusually rapid journey, Gus realised he still had five minutes before the witching hour. Someone put an arm around his waist and gave him an affectionate squeeze.

Her perfume identified her without Gus having to turn around.

"It may never happen, Gus," whispered Vera Butler. "Cheer up."

"I've just spoken to Divya," said Gus. "She smells trouble too. Why is everyone so quiet? Kassie waved instead of hollering a greeting across the mezzanine. That alone would make anyone nervous."

"The PCC was waiting for Kenneth outside his office when he arrived. They've been shut in there ever since."

"Does that mean I've had a wasted journey?" asked Gus. "I brought the files on another successful case, hoping to get the boss's week off to a good start."

"Kenneth phoned me earlier to add items to the lunch order," said Vera. "I think the PCC intends to join you."

Gus spotted Geoff Mercer's office door opening.

"If I hide behind Geoff, perhaps the PCC won't realise I'm there," he said.

"Get on with you," laughed Vera. "We'll be in later with your lunch. At times like this, I remember a piece of advice my father gave me. He told me he'd always listen to what was being said, and no matter how much he didn't like the news, he'd count to ten before speaking."

"Did he ever find it useful?" asked Gus.

"Hard to tell," said Vera. "He admitted he usually hit the person before he reached ten."

Gus caught up with Geoff as he reached the Chief Constable's door.

"Can you tell me what's going on, Geoff?" he asked.

"I'm as much in the dark as everyone else," said Geoff. "I don't think it will be long before we both find out. I do have news of my own, though."

Geoff knocked before Gus could grill him, and Kenneth

invited them in. He wasn't standing by the window this morning but sat beside the PCC at his desk. Gus knew Geoff Mercer had met Stuart Midwinter before, but this was the first time he'd seen their supremo in the flesh.

Gus remembered reading that Midwinter was a year older than he was and had lived and worked in Devizes all his life. He had retired from a local solicitor's office to take up his current role. Ninety grand a year from the Home Office would encourage plenty of people to join in the fun.

Midwinter's background explained why he seemed so at ease when appearing on local television or answering questions from reporters on the steps outside this building. Smooth was the first word that came to mind. He was someone who couldn't stop themselves from getting their name and face in the media.

One of his latest photo opportunities had been after the renaming of a lane in the sleepy village a few miles from Devizes, where he lived with his wife, Tessa. Midwinter had received a letter from a single resident complaining that the name, Pepper Lane, was inappropriate as it had links to a Jamaican plantation from the eighteenth century. Nobody from the village was aware whether that was how the lane had got its name in the first place and thought the link tenuous, but residents awoke one morning to find that overnight Pepper Lane had become Green Lane, sporting a new, black and white sign.

Stuart Midwinter was interviewed that evening on BBC Points West, suited and booted, all smiles, clutching a frisky King Charles Spaniel to his chest. Gus remembered being glad he and Suzie hadn't eaten.

Today, the PCC was wearing another expensive, dark blue suit over a light blue shirt, plus a tie so noticeable it had to represent a college, club, or society Gus would never get invited to join. While studying the man who held the future of everyone in the room in his hands, he realised that he'd started to speak to him.

"My role is to be the voice of the people and hold the police to account," said Stuart Midwinter. "I'm responsible for the totality of policing, and I aim to cut crime and deliver an effective and efficient police service within the Wiltshire police force area. We've made progress in the past two years, but Kenneth and I agreed that more needs to be done, and after forty years of loyal service, it's time for him to step aside."

"Kenneth knew the appointment was only ever temporary," said Gus. "Some might say he should have had the top job earlier, but we march to a different beat these days."

"Quite," said the PCC.

"When will the change take place?" asked Geoff Mercer.

"I prefer a gradual process," said Midwinter. "It has been an enjoyable time working closely with Kenneth. We will continue to work closely together on our shared goal of making Wiltshire safer until the first of April next year. My task was to find the next Chief Constable of Wiltshire Police, and an early start has allowed me to carry out a well-planned recruitment process to get the right person to lead the force into the future."

"Applications have been invited from eligible candidates from Assistant Chief Constables and equivalent ranks," said Kenneth. "Successful applicants were shortlisted, and interviews were held by an independent panel, chaired by Mr Midwinter."

"My mission since I took office has been to work in partnership with Kenneth to make our county a safer place to live, work and visit," said the PCC. "To achieve this, we need a quality policing service which meets the needs of our communities and is trusted by our residents. So I searched for the right person to drive this ambition forward."

"We're only too aware that dedicated, ethical, operationally experienced and focused leaders are thin on the ground," said Kenneth. "Stuart believes he's found someone who can quickly earn our officers' and staff's confidence and respect - from the executive level to the frontline."

"An inspirational leader to lead Wiltshire Police into the future," said Midwinter. "They will place great emphasis on getting the basics right: ensuring our force delivers quality police investigations, improves outcomes and justice for victims, and tackles those crimes that matter most to our communities."

"The right candidate will have a proven track record of delivering high-performing services, leading organisational change and fighting crime," said Gus. "But also working closely with local authorities and partner agencies to deliver effective community safety partnerships and a policing service that our residents want - and deserve."

"You have a better grasp of the situation than I gave you credit for, Mr Freeman," said Midwinter.

"I've read the pamphlets, Mr Midwinter," said Gus, "and a photographic memory helps. So I imagine you're close to announcing the name of Kenneth's successor?"

"We both agree ACC Sylvia Robbins from Durham ticked every box on our wish list," said Midwinter. "She was by far the best candidate we saw."

"Sylvia has agreed to join us here at London Road from January the first," said Kenneth. "After what we hope will be a smooth handover, I'll retire at the end of March."

Gus looked across at Geoff Mercer.

"You're quiet, Geoff," he said.

"I was half-expecting this news," said Geoff. "As it happens, the timing couldn't have been better. Christine and I have finally sold our house and can move forward with our move to Clench Common. I don't know whether ACC Robbins will want me around for the entire handover period. I'll start the ball rolling today, and perhaps I can retire at the end of February if that's acceptable, Kenneth?"

"I see no reason to object," said Midwinter.

Kenneth Truelove raised an eyebrow. Gus wondered whether he was counting to ten.

"We'll do everything we can to accommodate you, Mercer," said Kenneth.

"Thank you, sir," said Geoff.

Gus waited for someone to speak, but all was silence.

Kenneth glanced at the clock and took the opportunity to ring Vera.

"Lunch is on its way," he said when he put the phone down. "While we're waiting, perhaps you could fill us in on the contents of that folder you're clutching, Freeman."

"Another cold case solved, sir," said Gus. "Matthew Archer, a delivery driver for the Jade Garden Restaurant in Haydon Wick, Swindon, was murdered in February 2009. We've identified his killer as James Hatch, a thug working for a London wholesaler, Gabriel Rollins. The Liang family, who owned the restaurant, were pressured into switching suppliers through intimidatory tactics employed by the firm Rollins operates. The original owner and his wife have retired to France, but their two children have continued running the restaurant and takeaway. A nasty business, sir, where the daughter has been forced to sleep with Rollins to prevent an escalation in costs that would bankrupt her and her older brother."

"Why was this chap Archer killed?" asked the PCC.

"Archer and the owner's son were both handling deliveries in 2009," said Gus. "Hatch wouldn't have known who was driving to the remote address where they chose to carry out the attack. The message to the Liang family was loud and clear. Like many other takeaways and restaurants that Rollins and his crew approached, fall in line, or else."

"Nine years ago, you say?" said the PCC. "We must be thankful the county has far fewer murders now."

"The intimidation, threats, and assault have continued until last weekend," said Gus.

"Quite. When will our people get this Hatch character before a judge and jury, Mr Freeman?"

"The Met have arrested Rollins and Hatch and are running the show now. I was tasked with discovering who killed Matthew Archer and why. Job done. DS Mercer will ensure the Met gets the necessary evidence to support the case they prepare for the Crown Prosecution Service. Rollins has a wholesale delivery business with over a hundred food outlets on his books. So I imagine there's plenty of work to be done between here and London to snare all the victims. Indeed, the crime wave might travel further west."

"A complex operation then," said Midwinter. "It might not be possible to take advantage of any successful outcome before Kenneth takes his leave."

"The wheels of justice grind extremely slowly," said Gus. "With your background, you must have had first-hand experience, sir."

"Quite. Clench Common is a popular spot, DS Mercer. Tessa and I looked at houses in that village a few years ago, but nothing came on the market within our price range."

"Christine and I wished to downsize," said Geoff. "I

don't imagine our little cottage would have been among the properties your estate agent sent you."

Gus was impressed at the speed with which Midwinter had changed the subject. He guessed it had been covered in Media Training 101. After all, Police and Crime Commissioners were politicians in all but name, with bosses sitting behind a desk in the Home Office. When was the last time a politician answered a direct question?

A knock at the door scuppered any further discussion on the justice system. Vera and Kassie entered the room after the customary indistinct invitation from the Chief Constable and quickly placed the correct food and drink order in front of the four men.

"Enjoy," said Kassie as she turned her trolley and headed soundlessly to the door. Vera smiled and winked at Gus as she walked past. Wonders will never cease, thought Gus.

Stuart Midwinter sipped his milky coffee and inspected his sandwich.

"This looks good," he said. "Egg and cress with a dash of mayonnaise."

"The firm who won the contract offers a good service at a competitive cost," said Kenneth. "I believe you'll find this works out cheaper in the long run. We don't have staff disappearing off-site on extended lunches anymore."

"You would struggle to get to a fast-food outlet, get served, and get back in thirty minutes," said Geoff Mercer. "It was doable when we allowed everyone an hour for lunch."

Gus spotted Stuart Midwinter watching Geoff devouring his bacon bap. Maybe the egg and cress didn't look so good now. Gus finished his wrap and black coffee and waited for the others.

"It's temporary, Gus," said Geoff. "The person originally assigned that task was rushed to the hospital with appendicitis at the weekend, meaning Lydia will work in Swindon with Raj Sengupta until Christmas. She will rejoin the team in the New Year, when, all things being equal, the other DS will be back, fit as a fiddle."

"My day gets better and better," said Gus. "Is there anything else you want to tell me, sir?"

The Chief Constable shuffled in his seat.

"The CPS has contacted me," he said. "Ahmet Tekin has opted to plead not guilty, despite the overwhelming evidence against him. As a result, his case will be heard at Swindon Crown Court starting on Wednesday."

"The name doesn't register," said Midwinter. "Was he one of the Albanian gangsters who threatened to kill you, Freeman?"

"No, he's a Turkish barber," said Gus. "He murdered a young woman in Swindon seven years ago. Laura Mallinder's death was one of the first cold cases we handled. DS Mercer passed the relevant files to Gablecross for them to prepare the case for the CPS."

"I presume they failed to identify the killer in the first place," said Midwinter.

"That's how we were set up to operate," said Gus. "Kenneth selects a historical case that had to be abandoned due to a lack of suspects, evidence, or resources. Then, we take another look, and if we're successful this time around, we allow detectives from the original police area to get the win. The system has two benefits. First, detectives who worked on the case and have been kept awake at night fretting over what they might have missed finally get closure. Then those who screwed up can be dealt with if they're still in post."

"With some historical cases, you must encounter detectives that have retired," said Midwinter. "Little can be done in that instance, I imagine?"

"We can ensure their previously glowing reputation gets tarnished," said Gus. "We're not on a witch hunt, though, Mr Midwinter. Our prime concern is the family of the victim. Nothing will ever bring back their loved one, but when a murder remains unsolved for a decade or more, it means we've let them down."

"Quite," said Midwinter.

"Why did the CPS contact you, sir?" Gus asked Kenneth. "It's never happened before."

"You've handed them a series of winnable cases, Freeman," said the Chief Constable. "I was told to ask you to invite team members who worked on the Mallinder case to attend. They wished to show their gratitude and allow you to watch justice being done. "

"How long do they believe the case will last?" asked Gus.

"You know it's never wise to speculate, Gus," said Geoff Mercer. "There's no such thing as a typical murder trial. My best guess is that you shouldn't go backwards and forwards to Swindon for more than ten days."

"Lydia won't be available," said Gus. "That leaves my two Detective Sergeants."

"DS Hardy and DS Davis," said Kenneth. "It will be a good experience for them. Although, I imagine both have given evidence in court in the past. Seeing the whole proceedings from start to finish as a spectator will be different."

"I hope Melody Davis allows her husband to hang around for the inevitable guilty verdict," said Gus. "Their first child is due early in December. We knew Neil would be taking paternity leave in the coming weeks, but we're faced with a different scenario. So why didn't Tekin plead guilty?"

"The CPS and their legal team will discover that on Monday," said Kenneth.

"My concerns about the number of people in the office on Monday morning seem misplaced now," said Gus. "Grace and Blessing will be the only ones working."

Kenneth Truelove had another card to play.

"The emergency at Gablecross meant Ms Logan Barre would be absent for a month," he said. "I was sure you could have coped with another case before I got the call from the CPS. Once I realised three more of you could be away from your desks for a week or more, it made sense to find an assignment for DI Packenham and DC Umeh to undertake here at London Road."

"Agatha Christie," muttered Gus. "And then there were none."

"We have spoken about this before, Freeman," said Kenneth.

"I hadn't imagined it happening quite so quickly," said Gus. "What did you manage to get lined up for Grace and Blessing?"

"It was a no-brainer," said Geoff Mercer. "As soon as Kenneth told me I had two rising stars available who lived in the countryside, I suggested they supplement the team assigned to the Farm Watch initiative."

"Farm Watch is the police alert service that aims to spot and prevent rural crime," said Stuart Midwinter.

"I'm aware of the frequency with which criminals separate farmers from their vital large vehicles," said Gus. "Let alone their quad bikes. Perhaps because their daughter is a detective, the thieves have given my partner's parents' farm a miss in the past. Now those two rising detectives you mentioned are lodging at the farm; John Ferris can probably get his insurance premiums reduced."

"Quite," said the PCC. "Wiltshire has more than its fair share of farms and rural properties. There are so many opportunities for a determined criminal gang to access buildings far enough away from the main house for them not to be spotted. The free scheme sends members a message about criminal activity and advice tailored to their area. The Ferris family and others can tap into police information to help protect themselves and their property. For example, if a suspicious vehicle is spotted near a farm and reported, a message can be sent out to all farms nearby, urging them to be vigilant and check their property is safe."

"Will Grace and Blessing be touring the county?" asked Gus. He wondered whose car they would be using.

"I think we have enough addresses on our books to keep them tied up for two weeks, minimum," said Kenneth.

"We hope they can persuade more owners to join the scheme," said Geoff. "We need them to stress that under the scheme, they get crime prevention advice to ensure property and goods are secure, and a property marking scheme to make it harder for thieves to dispose of stolen goods. In addition, we'll supply them with warning signs for gates and property boundaries so criminals know the property is protected."

"We know CCTV cameras inside retail businesses and outside domestic properties can deter criminals," said the PCC. "This is a similar approach, where we do what we can to make the criminal think twice before attempting to steal a tractor, or quad bike, from farms that display the items that suggest they're security conscious."

"I'm sure you're right," said Gus. "Have I heard everything now?"

"In due course, you'll return to pick up the details of your next case, Freeman," said the Chief Constable. "I can't put a date on it, but if you need something to cheer you up, it will mean returning to your old stamping ground. A double murder in Salisbury, investigated by your colleagues at Bourne Hill nick in 2012."

"Not Spider Crees?" asked Gus.

Kenneth nodded.

"John Crees and Mandy Howard, members of the biker community."

"Why did you refer to him as Spider, Mr Freeman?" asked the PCC.

"A series of tattoos," said Gus. "On his body, face, leather jacket, and the frame of his Harley Davidson."

"You were otherwise engaged," said Geoff Mercer. "A string of sexual assaults near the college."

"Five young women were attacked as they left evening classes during September and December 2012," said Gus. "As I was tied up with that business, DI Phil Crocker led the murder investigation. His second-in-command would have been DS Bob Mears. We barely saw one another until the end of January, but they hadn't had any joy with the people John Crees ran with. They've got a code that makes omerta sound like the cub scouts' promise."

"I promise to do my best, be kind and helpful, and love our world," said Stuart Midwinter.

Gus resisted the temptation to offer a one-word response.

"All potential leads were followed," said Geoff Mercer. "Nothing was found that justified extending the investigation, and it was closed down. A previous Chief Constable dismissed it as an internal dispute among the local Hells Angels community."

"Don't worry about the Salisbury case for now, Freeman," said Kenneth. "It's been in my drawer since you returned to the fold, and it can wait until you and the team can give it your full attention."

"Understood, sir," said Gus. "Might I ask who will work in the office from next Monday?"

"Morris Beard, Rosie Allison, and Sarah Holland," said the PCC. "Morris is the Strategic Delivery Lead for Prevention and Youth. Rosie and Sarah are two passionate individuals who support Morris in delivering improvements and driving forward the partnership's work within the portfolio area."

I'm sure I'll find time between now and when we meet to discover what that meant, thought Gus. He made a mental note to ask Suzie to translate it tonight.

"I don't think we need to keep you two any longer," said the Chief Constable. "We'll keep you updated on our progress."

"It was good to meet you, Mr Freeman," said the PCC. "Keep up the good work."

# Chapter Two

GEOFF AND GUS left the room and headed for Geoff's office.

"I knew things were going too well this morning," said Gus once they were behind a closed door.

"Try to remember what I said, Gus," said Geoff. "It's a temporary setback. At the latest, you and your team will be back in harness in the New Year. If you play your cards right, you can wangle an office at Bourne Hill to make the best use of your time working on that double murder case. You won't be disturbed by Morris Beard and his cronies."

"You and Kenneth have the finishing line in sight," said Gus. "Mine is obscured by gathering clouds."

Geoff laughed.

"A tad dramatic," he said. "Sylvia Robbins doesn't take over the reins until the first of April. You can solve several cases before then. Enough to convince her she'd be a fool not to keep taking advantage of your experience. You might lose a team member here or there, but fresh blood will always become available. The PCC told you it was too soon to say what would happen in April. We can only be sure that Kenneth will pack his suitcase for a cruise, and I'll be helping Christine decorate our new home. Oh, and you'll be in Urchfont on paternity leave at some point in the month. There are many positives for each of us to look forward to next year."

"I'd better get back to the office," said Gus.

"If you see Kassie Trotter outside, can you check whether she was baking at the weekend? I didn't dare ask when we were in with Kenneth."

"You'll miss her cakes when you move to Clench Common," said Gus.

"Not a bit of it. I've followed Kenneth's lead," said Geoff. "Kassie says she will add me to her list for a Sunday delivery after I leave London Road."

"Good to know you've got your priorities right, Geoff," said Gus. "All you have to do now is work out how to make the order last until the following Sunday."

Gus left Geoff Mercer with a problem to solve and crossed the mezzanine to the top of the stairs. Vera and Kassie were nowhere to be seen.

"Typical," muttered Gus. "Not a sign of either of them."

He shuffled downstairs to the foyer, opened the front door, and walked the short distance to the Ford Focus. As he left the car park and drove towards the town centre, Gus spotted them returning from lunch. No doubt they had been at Vera's house for their thirty-minute escape.

Gus tried to attract their attention, but they were deep in conversation. There was nothing for it. He had to soldier on without the healing properties of a Chelsea bun or a cream horn. Forty minutes later, he parked beside Lydia's red Mini and waited for the lift to descend. It was time to face the music.

"Welcome back, guv," said Neil. "My money's on somewhere in the south of the county for our next case. Am I right?"

Gus looked around the room. He'd come to enjoy working here. A deep sigh gave the game away that everything was about to change.

"It's bad news, guv, isn't it," said Lydia.

Gus told them everything.

"I never saw that coming," said Neil.

"Which bit, Neil?" asked Alex. "The Chief Constable and DS Mercer leaving within weeks of one another, or Ahmet Tekin pleading not guilty?"

"The first two getting out while the going was good was always on the cards," said Neil. "As for the rest, it all qualifies as unexpected. I can't see how Tekin can dispute the murder weapon. It matched the wounds of the murder victim and was used by him when he attacked Theo Hickerton. He was just five yards from where I was standing. As for one of the PCC's teams moving in with us, it makes no sense. We're not exactly blessed with acres of spare space."

"It might not be too bad when the screens are in place," said Grace. "It could get crowded in the restroom, though."

"I hope they bring their own supplies of coffee and biscuits," said Neil.

"Grace and Blessing won't need to worry about that before Christmas," said Lydia. "They'll be based at London Road with a long list of farms to visit, to show them ways to keep their expensive equipment safe."

"No, it's you I feel sorry for, Lydia," said Neil. "Raj Sengupta isn't Mr Dynamite. Gablecross thought they'd got rid of him when he went to join the Met as a cybercrime team leader, but he returned within twelve months. DI Sengupta reckoned he didn't fit in in London, and they got him working on similar crimes in the West. He can do less damage that way. Raj won't stray far from the office, so you'll get plenty of exercise if there's any fetching and carrying to be done."

"I need to get a floor plan of Gablecross," said Lydia. "That building is a rabbit warren."

"Did the Chief Constable hint at what we'd be doing later in the month, or the New Year, guv?" asked Alex.

"Neil backed the right horse," said Gus. "We're off to Bourne Hill police station for a double murder on my old patch in 2012. I don't imagine that will be something to look forward to. A biker gang was involved, not a friendly bunch of people who go for a spin at the weekends. The sort that has amusing phrases attached to them."

"Three can keep a secret if two are dead, d'you mean, guv?" asked Alex.

"That's one of them," said Gus. "Another favourite is we don't conform, so the police harass us."

"When I was working in my old job, I witnessed several occasions where the local club staged positive demonstrations to convince the public they belonged to the ninety-nine percent," said Alex. "They'd make a big show of turning up at the hospital with toys for the kids at Christmas; that sort of thing."

"Why ninety-nine percent?" asked Blessing.

"For decades, there were stories about bikers being responsible for all manner of violent behaviour," said Gus. "Before I joined the police, the Rockers in the Fifties got a bad reputation. It harks back to the 'we don't conform' idea. For their part, official motorcycle organisations would stress that ninety-nine percent of riders were law-abiding, solid citizens. Only one percent were intent on causing trouble."

"That backfired," said Alex. "The one's intent on causing trouble adopted the one percent as a badge. As a result, you often see the one percent patch sewn onto their clothing."

"I remember the cavalcade of bikers who always arrived first at the war memorial in Wootton Bassett when bodies were being repatriated from Afghanistan," said Neil. "That always felt genuine. It goes to show you never can tell."

"Whether you think of them as gangs or motorcycle clubs, they're far more complex an organisation than you could ever imagine," said Gus. "As for the charitable exercises and the cavalcades, don't forget the rogue element is a tiny percentage."

"I can't imagine you in a grubby leather jacket, Alex," said Blessing.

"I never rode without a full set of leathers, Blessing," said Alex. "If my accident had occurred in the Fifties when helmets weren't compulsory, I wouldn't have stood a chance. Despite the protection that my leathers gave me, my injuries were extensive."

"All that trauma is behind you now, thank goodness," said Lydia.

"I've got you to thank for that," said Alex.

"I read there are around two dozen chartered motorcycle clubs in this country," said Gus. "You can't mistake the uniform - leather jackets that have seen better days and powerful motorcycles. The club usually has a meeting place where members can enjoy a party with loud music. These gangs don't often hit the news headlines. The Hells Angels, the biggest motorcycle club in the world, steadfastly maintain that, first and foremost, they're just a motorcycle club."

"You sound as if you had dealings with them, guv," said Neil.

"I wasn't involved in the double murder investigation, Neil," said Gus. "That pleasure fell to DI Crocker and DS Mears. I didn't bump into them often during the two months after the bodies were discovered, but when I did, Phil Crocker told me that they hadn't felt safe since."

"What do you mean, guv?" asked Neil. "Were they threatened?"

"It wasn't subtle, Neil," said Gus. "Phil Crocker told me fifteen to twenty bikes would ride past their houses, day and night, while they tried to gather evidence. There was little they could do. There were no phone calls or death threats in the post. If they asked traffic cops to find an excuse to pull a patched biker over, they never carried any weapons. They could issue a few fines for minor offences, but it didn't deter the intimidation. A decade before this double murder, Phil Crocker had seen reports from Scandinavia where motorcycle gangs not only had access to machine guns, hand grenades, and car bombs but were prone to using them. He was scared."

"I remember a TV report after an attack in Copenhagen, guv," said Alex. "That was a clash between two gangs. They weren't targeting the police with that rocket launcher."

"Not on that occasion, Alex," said Gus. "However, the Salisbury bikers allegedly involved in the murder were a law unto themselves. They had bought a house on the outskirts, close to the ring road, in 2002. It was an end terrace property. Nothing special, just a three-bedroom, one-bathroom family home. Within twelve months, the next-door neighbours moved out."

"They'd had enough of the partying and loud music," said Blessing.

"Motorbikes roaring up and down the street without regard for other people," said Grace. "Did the council do anything?"

"There wasn't much they could do," said Gus. "The neighbours never complained. It was private property, not social housing. Nobody asked where the money came from, but the gang members bought the vacant property and knocked through the walls downstairs and upstairs to convert the place into a clubhouse. Phil Crocker told me that people on the street reckoned the building had a fitted bar and a full-sized snooker table on the ground floor."

"Why didn't the police raid the clubhouse?" asked Neil.

"No laws were broken," said Gus, "and nobody ever complained about what was happening."

"They were too scared," said Lydia. "Do gang members still live at that address?"

"I don't have that information," said Gus. "The boss told me the case file would stay in his drawer until we could give it our full attention."

"No wonder you said this case wasn't something to look forward to, guv," said Neil. "A pity we handed back those stab vests we borrowed at Burnham-on-Sea. We might need them."

"Forewarned is forearmed, Neil," said Gus. "We'll ensure we carry out interviews at Bourne Hill police station. Then, if uniformed officers have to escort our guests from their homes, they can take the necessary precautions."

"And the risks," said Grace. "I feel safer already."

"Is there anything we need to do before we leave this evening, guv?" asked Lydia.

"We have squatters' rights to this end of the office," said

Gus. "I suggest you move your desks closer to mine. Don't give the people the PCC is sending here at the weekend any ideas. If there's a space at the far end of the room under the clock, they will use it. It's human nature."

At five o'clock, everyone took a last look around the office and travelled in the lift to the ground floor.

"Enjoy your day off, guv," said Neil when they reached their cars. "What time shall I pick you up on Wednesday morning?"

"Eight o'clock?" said Gus. "What about Alex?"

"I'll be taking him with me, guv," said Lydia. "I can drop him at the Crown Court building in Islington Street on my way to Gablecross."

"Of course," said Gus. "Good luck tomorrow, Lydia. Try not to fall out with Raj Sengupta. Although, be warned that he'll try the patience of a saint."

"Nothing to worry about then, guv," said Lydia. "I'm no saint."

Lydia's red Mini soon reversed out and shot towards the entrance. Neil wasn't far behind them. Gus waited for Blessing Umeh to ease her Nissan Micra out of the parking bay as Grace stood and watched.

"Don't forget your wellington boots, Grace," he called. "I know the ground will be frost-hardened at this time of year, but items left behind by farmyard animals can play havoc with your shoes."

Grace gave him a rueful smile.

"You didn't say much about what you feel about these upcoming arrangements, Gus," she said as she joined him by his car.

"It is what it is, Grace," said Gus. "Geoff Mercer tells me it's temporary. However, we both know what the powers-that-be are like. The PCC is responsible for how the

Wiltshire force operates, and he's keen for Sylvia Robbins to move in next week. He's got an agenda, and she will want to make a name for herself as soon as possible. We can only hope any final decisions aren't made until Kenneth has closed the door on his office at the end of March. I don't see any of you having anything to fear from what happens after that date. Rumours will soon start spreading on what the future holds for the Crime Review Team, but if my services are no longer required, I'll be the only real casualty. If there's a good time to be put out of a job, then April is the month I'd choose. I can work on my allotment until Suzie has the baby, and then I'm well-placed to let her get back to work as soon as she's ready."

"You've got it all worked out, haven't you?" said Grace.

"Pretty much," said Gus. "This job was always going to end in tears."

Blessing revved her engine.

"Your carriage awaits," said Gus. "Someone's keen to get back for dinner with Jackie."

"When will we see you again?" asked Grace. "Why don't we have a night at the Waggon & Horses on Friday week? It will be good to catch up before Christmas."

"Good thinking," said Gus. "I'll check with Suzie and then contact the rest of the team with the arrangements. But, unfortunately, we can't leave it until closer to Christmas because the pub will be heaving with customers, and Alex and Lydia are travelling to Scotland to spend the holidays with her mother."

Grace got into the passenger seat next to Blessing, and they were turning into Church Street as Gus started the Focus and set off for Urchfont. After another uneventful journey, Gus swung the Focus through the gateway and parked beside Suzie's Golf.

"Dinner's on its way," Suzie called. "I'm in the lounge."

Gus checked the kitchen for activity, but the room was in darkness.

"Did I miss something," said Gus. "We're not going out tonight, are we?"

"No, I wanted to chat about your day," said Suzie. "I've ordered your favourite Chinese meal."

"It feels like the last request of a prisoner on Death Row," said Gus. "I can't see the PCC or Kenneth spilling the beans. So, who talked?"

"I was at school with Sarah Holland," said Suzie. "We joined the Pony Club on the same night and have always been close. Sarah can't keep anything secret, so when she heard her team was moving to the Old Police Station office, she rang me."

"The PCC seems to think we're living in the lap of luxury," said Gus. "Another three people won't be that much of a hardship, especially if they're off-site most of the time. I might change my opinion if they have naughty school children traipsing past our crime scene photos with their parents."

"I don't think that's likely, darling," said Suzie. "That was all Sarah could tell me, but she did say they would be able to settle in while you and the team were absent."

"The CPS contacted Kenneth," said Gus. "They invited us to attend Crown Court for the trial of Ahmet Tekin, the man who murdered Laura Mallinder. Neil's picking me up at eight on Wednesday morning. Lydia has been transferred to Gablecross to cover maternity leave in the cybercrime section, so we won't need to worry about Alex making it to the court on time."

"What about Grace and Blessing?" asked Suzie.

"Farm Watch," said Gus.

"Uniforms and PCSOs do most of the leg work on that scheme," said Suzie. "It's beneath a Detective Inspector. They must want Grace to take over from Richard Wallis."

"Is he a DI, too?" asked Gus.

Suzie nodded.

"Go on, you may as well tell me," said Gus.

"DI Wallis was accused of inappropriate touching and conversation with a junior member of police staff at a social event in Trowbridge," said Suzie. "He faces a misconduct hearing at Portishead on Thursday."

"I've never heard of the guy," said Gus. "Has he been with us long?"

"Three years," said Suzie. "He transferred from Hampshire as a training officer. After that, our paths have rarely crossed, and only in the past year has he spent time at London Road."

"I remember Dominic Culverhouse's hearing," said Gus. "I imagine this one will follow a similar protocol."

"Yes, it will be held behind closed doors with members of the public and press banned from attending."

"As I thought, just like Culverhouse," said Gus. "Not that it did him any good, but questions are always asked if anything leaks about the case. Someone screams cover-up. The medical profession gets accused of the same thing, that they're sweeping mistakes under the carpet, hoping the public never learns the truth."

"Our MP has criticised the private hearing," said Suzie. "She told the press it was clearly in the public interest to hear the full facts of the case."

"I don't recall voting in a by-election," said Gus. "Leonard Pemberton Smythe has been out of the picture for nine months, but our world hasn't stopped spinning. He was still on remand the last time I heard."

"A seat in the House of Commons automatically becomes vacant if its MP receives a prison sentence of twelve months or more," said Suzie. "Your pen-friend Joyce will see her husband go down for over a year. I heard a whisper last week that the CPS will be ready to move forward early next year. In normal circumstances, a writ would be issued to the local returning officer within three months of the seat becoming vacant. They can then go ahead with arranging a by-election. But, as Leonard's case was far from normal, and the General Election was only last year, they asked MPs from the neighbouring constituencies to take turns standing in. Once the trial ends, we'll vote for the next cab off the rank. The successful candidate could have three years to make their mark."

"Devizes has had a Tory MP for almost a century," said Gus. "It's not a seat which a rising star from any other parties would wish to get selected to contest."

"The local MP looking after our interests felt strongly that Richard Wallis should face the court of public opinion," said Suzie. "I can see her point."

"The panel will be invited to publish the outcome of the hearing," said Gus, "but it's not certain they would. The officer's name, whether any standards were breached, or any finding of gross misconduct was reached, all that detail could be withheld. The MP will undoubtedly appear on TV on Thursday evening, claiming the public has the right to know. The panel might decide that even a brief statement about the outcome wasn't required."

"The charge sheet indicated the conversation breached standards of professional behaviour relating to equality, diversity, authority, respect, and courtesy," said Suzie.

"A full set," said Gus. "Even without the inappropriate touching, you would think Wallis's feet won't touch the floor on his way out of the police force. What reason did we give this MP for denying a public hearing?"

"Our Media department stressed a private hearing was necessary because of the law relating to the anonymity of complainants following allegations of a sexual offence. We want to encourage the reporting of alleged wrongdoing, and public hearings can deter victims from coming forward. A private hearing protects the rights of witnesses and their families, including those of the officer concerned."

"I suppose Wallis has been suspended on full pay?" asked Gus.

"Since late September," said Suzie. "That's in line with police regulations, pending the outcome of the investigation. I hadn't heard his name mentioned for the past couple of months. However, someone must have spoken to the MP because another rumour spread around the building today. Evidently, Wallis had been in trouble in Hampshire. He was alleged to have been domineering, controlling, and physically abusive to two women while training new officers back in 2015."

"Hampshire decided a game of 'pass the parcel' was in order," said Gus. "Wiltshire was lumbered with a problem cop, and if the MP wasn't in with a chance of making a few headlines before, she was once she heard from the whistle blower."

"The Chief Constable was asked to comment by a reporter from the Chronicle," said Suzie. "That article appeared in the newspaper this morning. He told them he had met with the two women involved in the case from 2015 to hear their experiences first-hand and apologised on behalf of Hampshire & Isle of Wight Police. He said he had worked hard to make a difference to the force's culture on all discriminatory practices, and that work would continue to ensure a safe and professional workplace for everyone."

"I can see the PCC and Kenneth getting their stories straight over the next couple of days," said Gus. "Whatever they say won't satisfy everyone."

"You can please some of the people some of the time," said Suzie.

"Quite," said Gus. "Curse that man. He's got me at it now."

"Who?" asked Suzie.

"Stuart Midwinter, it's his favourite word. He uses it like a full-stop to change the subject."

The front doorbell rang.

"Grab the lap trays from the kitchen," said Suzie. "The cutlery's there too. That will be our evening meal being delivered."

Suzie answered the door while Gus retrieved the items from the kitchen table.

Thirty minutes later, he was placing the containers in the appropriate bin.

"That was a good choice," he said. "Coffee, darling?"

"Yes, please. Did the PCC's news prevent you from collecting a new case?"

Gus returned to the lounge with two coffees, and they made themselves comfortable on the settee.

"Kenneth tempted me with a quick glimpse of the murder file," said Gus. "You may remember it? A double murder in Salisbury in 2012, where a biker and his girl-friend were found, dead, in bed."

"John Crees," said Suzie. "A face only a mother could love. What was the girlfriend's name? I've forgotten."

"Amanda Howard, known as Mandy. It was thought Spider and Mandy fell out with the local motorcycle fraternity. Because I only got a few snippets from the detectives involved at Bourne Hill at the time, I know little more than that. Do you have any insight on the case?"

"I was a novice DS, working out of London Road," said Suzie. "We didn't need to cross the Plain too often to offer a helping hand. My boss then was Mark Colbourne, one of the current Assistant Chief Constables. He heard stories from the detective in charge that convinced him we were better off out of it."

"Phil Crocker," said Gus. "The local gang harassed him and his Sergeant. More than a dozen bikes roared up and down the street outside their houses."

"We know where you live," said Suzie. "Chilling. My brothers rode bikes when they were younger. More like Alex Hardy than the 'live young, die fast' brigade. Dad put his foot down when they wanted to ride up to Long Marston near Stratford-upon-Avon for the Bulldog Bash one year. Despite being organised by the Hells Angels, the event was open to all bikers. It featured circuit and drag bike racing, motorcycle stunts, rock bands, food, and plenty of beer."

"The police tried to get the Bash event closed down," said Gus. "Although the festival was well-organised, they suspected the event was a magnet for organised crime."

"Yes," said Suzie. "The Bulldog Bash never caused Warwickshire Police much trouble, compared to other events attracting fifty thousand people. There were no police patrols at the site or personal searches conducted by police. The Hells Angels maintained security inside the festival grounds themselves. They won't have to worry about it anymore because the site was sold for a housing development last year. I wonder what John Crees did to annoy the Angels?"

"We'll have to wait to find out," said Gus. "Who knows? It might have been something else entirely."

"I'll make sure you're out of bed before I leave for work in the morning," said Suzie. "The sooner you start, the sooner you finish. I'll pin a list of chores on the notice board in the kitchen. Can you please pop into town to pick up my dry cleaning too?"

"It will be practice for next year," said Gus. "What would you like me to cook you for dinner?"

"Well, one of the reasons for the Chinese takeaway tonight was because I wanted to hear your news, but another was a lack of alternatives in the fridge or freezer. So we need to replenish our stocks."

"The allotment doesn't provide us with an abundance of fresh material at this time of year," said Gus. "I'll think of something to tickle your tastebuds. Then, on Wednesday evening, we'll eat at the Lamb."

"How's Melody?" asked Suzie, resting her right hand on her stomach.

"Counting the days, as is Neil," said Gus. "If he's lucky, Melody will go into labour and give him an excuse to leave the Crown Court on the first day. That reminds me, Amazing Grace suggested we had an evening at the Waggon & Horses on Friday the seventh of December."

"Is Grace your self-appointed social secretary now," said Suzie. "My, how she's changed. Oh, there it goes again."

"Sorry, darling, did I miss something?" asked Gus.

Suzie took hold of his hand and rested it on her stomach.

"I'm a little over twenty weeks," she said, "I thought I felt my first kick a few minutes ago. Then, another followed when I mentioned Grace."

Gus sat patiently but couldn't feel a thing.

"You can arrange that night out with the team," said Suzie. "I'll drive."

"We might not have Neil there," said Gus. "Melody's due any day now."

"There will still be enough of us to make it a good night. Although, it will be odd not to have Luke there."

"True, but he's made his choice," said Gus. "Time to move on. Nothing stays the same forever. Is there anything worth watching on TV tonight, or can we listen to music?"

"Give me a number between one and thirty-three," said Suzie.

"I didn't think we had that many vinyl albums," said Gus. "I hope you haven't added more of your middle-of-the-road stuff. That reduces the odds of me getting to hear something I love."

"I counted them at the weekend and haven't added anything lately. Number?"

"Seventeen," said Gus. "Do you want me to do the honours?"

"Please. I'm waiting for another kick."

Gus knelt by the rack of albums and found the middle one.

"I should have known," he muttered. "Joni Mitchell's second album."

"But you love that," said Suzie.

"Clouds," said Gus. "I've experienced enough of those for one day."

"Come here and give me a cuddle," said Suzie. "We'll watch the news and have an early night instead."

# Chapter Three

**Tuesday, 27 November 2018**

SUZIE WAS in the shower when Gus awoke. A glance at the clock on the bedside table as he strolled to the kitchen showed it was twenty-to-eight. While he made the coffee and decided what they could have for breakfast, he checked the list of chores pinned to the calendar.

"No," said Suzie. "I haven't added anything since last night. What's for breakfast?"

"We both need something warming," said Gus. "What do you say to porridge?"

"It's better than nothing, I suppose," said Suzie. "Go on, then. We haven't got time for much else. I'll pour the coffee. Did you manage to get much sleep last night?"

"No, I'm sorry if I disturbed you," Gus said. "I had so much on my mind."

"Whatever happens, you can't blame yourself," said Suzie. "Well, I suppose you could have told Kenneth you weren't interested in returning to work nine months ago, but since you did, nobody can question the success you've had."

"Team work," said Gus. "I was fortunate to get the three people I did when I started. After that, I was soon back in the swing of things, and whoever joined us slotted into the groove, and we never lost that initial impetus."

"Even Amazing Grace, despite your fears that she was out to get you," said Suzie. "I need to get ready for work. Have you decided where to start on that list of chores?"

"The ground will be too hard for me to tackle the allotment," said Gus. "I know, it's not on the list. But, if I'm stuck in Swindon Crown Court for days, Bert Penman will chastise me for not keeping up with everything he manages, even at his age. So I'll follow you into Devizes, visit the supermarket first, collect your dry cleaning, and have a haircut. That should make me presentable for our night out next week. Then, after tidying this place, I'll wander down to the allotment."

At twenty-five past eight, they stood beside their cars.

"There's definitely a nip in the air," said Suzie, as they both used a scraper on their windscreen.

"It's almost December," said Gus. "Why are we surprised? Take it steady in the lane in case it's icy. I'll see you tonight."

Suzie led the way through the gateway and resisted the temptation to roar ahead. As she carried on to London Road, Gus gave her a wave and turned into the Morrison's car park. He collected a trolley and joined dozens of early shoppers. If this were a sign of things to come, perhaps he and Suzie would order online and get their shopping delivered.

Gus returned to Urchfont by ten-thirty, happy he'd successfully ticked three items from Suzie's list. He treated himself to coffee and a slice of toast and studied the basket of fresh vegetables by the back door. With a thick slice of wholemeal bread, a bowl of soup would set him up for a couple of hours working on the allotment. So, with two more chores behind him, and central heating from lunch, he set off down the lane.

The sun had broken through, and although the temperature hadn't soared to double figures, it was warm enough to encourage him to start his winter digging. Unfortunately, there was no sign of Bert on the adjoining patch, and the Reverend had other things on her mind these days, so Gus resigned himself to working alone. After digging for thirty minutes, he cleared the weeds from the rest of his plot and harvested Brussels sprouts, a winter cabbage, plus a handful of leeks and parsnips. As Gus carried his haul back to the bungalow, he spotted the landlord of the Lamb walking from the pub car park. He called out to him.

"We'll be in tomorrow night at about eight," said Gus. "Will that be okay?"

"Table for four? No problem. I've been into Devizes since ten o'clock, so I don't know whether Bert's been in the pub, but we haven't seen him since Friday, Mr Freeman."

"That dose of flu knocked Bert and Irene sideways," said Gus. "Brett will be with us tomorrow evening. If anything untoward had happened, Brett would have rung."

"You're probably right," said the landlord. "Only Bert's eighty-something, and they can go downhill fast."

"Duly noted," said Gus. "See you tomorrow."

Gus walked through the gateway and approached the bungalow. Why hadn't he noticed the bushes on this side of the garden needed pruning? He'd dealt with the ones at the back when he had been on holiday a few weeks ago. Tess's rambling roses could do with a tidy-up too.

Gus had to put his vegetables on the doorstep while he found his door key, and once he'd replenished the basket by the back door, he searched for his sharpest set of secateurs —no time like the present. The light was fading fast, but he battled on, knowing he'd gone above and beyond today. Suzie could have no complaints.

All he had to do was decide what to cook tonight, and he had plenty of options now from his well-stocked kitchen.

### Wednesday, 28 November 2018

"NEIL WILL BE HERE IN A MINUTE," shouted Suzie. "Get a move on."

"The short hairs on the right-hand side of my head refuse to stick down," said Gus.

"You should have gone to the Turkish barber," said Suzie. "They don't leave enough at the sides to matter."

Gus emerged from the bedroom.

"It doesn't look that bad," said Suzie. "Are you sure you want to wear that shirt with that suit?"

"I'd rather not be going," said Gus. "That sounds like Neil outside, so it's too late to change now. Bye."

Gus grabbed a coat, kissed Suzie on the top of the head as she finished her second coffee, and headed outside.

"See you tonight, darling," called Suzie.

Gus slid into the passenger seat beside Neil Davis.

"Any news, Neil?" he asked.

"I had to leave the car running on the driveway for ten minutes before leaving home, guv," said Neil. "As for Melody, nothing yet. Her mother's with her. So, if the balloon goes up, she'll text me."

"You can leave the court whenever you like, Neil," said Gus.

"Cheers, guv," said Neil. "I thought we'd head for Avebury on the back roads, but things were tricky on the way here. So it might be safer to head for London Road and stay on the main roads to Wroughton. I bet Lydia and Alex will leave home ten minutes later and use the M4."

"As long as we're all there by nine o'clock, Neil, and in one piece, I don't mind."

Gus needn't have worried. Neil got them outside the Crown Court building by ten to nine.

"There are never many spare parking bays, guv," said Neil. "I'll park on Prince's Street. I can't see Lydia's Mini anywhere. Perhaps she's already dropped Alex outside the court."

Two minutes later, they were inside the main entrance. Experience had told Gus to leave certain items behind, as they had to negotiate security akin to that at an airport. He stood while someone swept his body with a hand-held scanner. When he cleared security, Gus found Neil studying the refreshments on offer from a row of vending machines.

"You've only just had breakfast, Neil," said Gus.

"It always pays to plan ahead, guv," said Neil. "I've spotted Alex, and he's just starting his security check. They were cutting it fine."

Gus led the way up the stairs to the first floor. He checked the noticeboard. The murder trial was in Court One.

"The Public Gallery and Media sit on the right, Neil," said Gus. "In case you've forgotten."

"The court clerk looks ready to bring matters to order, guv," said Neil. "The main feature will be on in a tick."

Alex soon entered the room and took a seat beside Neil.

"Morning, guv," whispered Alex. "Have you seen anyone you recognise?"

"Maggie Monk was coming out of the Ladies when we went through security," said Gus.

Several familiar faces entered the room and took their seats in front of the team. Gus had deliberately opted to sit with his back to the wall, so he could see everyone that mattered.

"My mate, Jake Latimer's arrived, guv," said Neil.

"I should hope so too, Neil," said Alex.

Gus watched the time-honoured procedures unfold. Everyone stood as the judge, James Denmark QC, took his seat. Members of the prosecution and defence teams gathered on either side of the room. Ahmet Tekin was escorted in and seated on the left-hand side of the judge. Gus thought he looked thinner in the face than when he'd last seen him, but he was smartly dressed, and his demeanour showed no lack of confidence.

The court clerk then asked Tekin's defence team whether the defendant was ready for trial. After he received confirmation, he walked to a side door and called out a series of random numbers. The appropriate juror was shown to the jury box when their panel number was called. The defence team rejected nobody who had been selected, so the jury was sworn in.

Ivor Kendrick, the counsel for the prosecution, then presented his case, and before long, Maggie Monk was in the witness box. First, she told the court how she'd found Laura's body. Later, the girl her clients had known as Camille told how she and Laura had worked together that evening until the last customer left. Her late husband had been ill, which meant she had left Laura alone after eight forty-five.

Ian Hewson was next to be called. He looked tanned and fitter than Gus remembered. The barrister asked Hewson what time he arrived at Gentle Touch that night.

"It was five to nine," said Hewson. "I looked at the clock on the wall at the top of the stairs after Laura let me in."

"What happened next?" asked Kendrick.

"She tidied her room, put towels into the washing machine, and moved other stuff into the tumble dryer."

"Why did you go to see her?" asked Kendrick.

"I wanted her to quit working at Gentle Touch," said Hewson. "We had been good together once, and I wanted her back. We argued. Laura told me she didn't want to be with anyone; she was happy being alone, and had no responsibilities. She said it was a mistake letting me in. I ran downstairs, slammed the door behind me, and drove home."

"Did you see anyone when you left?" asked Kendrick.

"There was a light in the barber shop on the ground floor. I'd been there for a haircut once. It seemed odd there would be someone working on a Sunday night, but I didn't see anyone."

"I can't see where this is headed, guv," said Neil. "Hewson might be a jerk, but he didn't kill Laura. His car was caught on an M4 camera at a time, meaning he left the parlour by ten past nine at the latest."

The prosecution barrister described the sequence of events following Hewson's departure. Ahmet Tekin had been downstairs in his barber shop and had let himself into the parlour with keys he had retained after leasing the first-floor space to Maggie Monk. He found Laura crying. Hewson, the ex-boyfriend, had trashed the room before he left.

Ivor Kendrick went on to explain how Tekin had previously showered Ms Mallinder with gifts of flowers and frequently asked her to go on a date with him. Laura had never indicated she was interested, but Tekin was besotted. When she laughed at the suggestion they could be a couple, the defendant stabbed her repeatedly with a makeshift weapon. He kept half of a favourite pair of scissors in his pocket, something he told police he always carried.

Ivor Kendrick showed the weapon to the jury in a clear plastic bag, entered into evidence as Exhibit A.

"Why haven't they mentioned the attack on DI Hickerton, guv?" asked Neil.

"It occurred almost seven years after the murder, Neil," said Gus. "The CPS believe they have a strong case and have thrown all their eggs into one basket."

"But we didn't find the murder weapon until that day," said Alex.

Gus only half-heard the rest of Ivor Kendrick's speech.

He was starting to see a small cloud forming on the horizon.

The counsel for the defence, Robin Burchell, made his opening statement, saying he would show that although Ahmet Tekin was in love with Laura Mallinder, he could not have killed her with the weapon introduced into evidence by the prosecution. He was adamant that the police could not prove that weapon was in his client's possession in June 2011.

Everyone in the gallery, whether from the media or members of the public, sat up straighter in their seats and realised they had a game on. The trial might not be as cut-and-dried as they thought. Backwards and forwards went the cross-court rallies, as Ivor Kendrick pointed out that although the weapon had never been found in the original investigation, the wounds caused by the makeshift weapon were so distinctive there could be no doubt this was the murder weapon.

Ivor Kendrick reminded the jury Tekin had agreed the half-scissors were his. Even though they'd broken, he kept them to remind him of the first barber shop he opened over twenty years earlier.

Robin Burchell asked how the weapon had been discovered after so much time had elapsed.

Kendrick explained that the defendant used it to attack DI Theo Hickerton on the eighth of May this year. Other officers had accompanied DI Hickerton to the first floor of Tekin's premises in Broadgreen. After Ms Mallinder's death, the massage parlour closed for good, and Ahmet Tekin moved his barber shop upstairs, opening a nail bar on the ground floor. When questioned by DI Hickerton, he replied that he had arrived at the shop at seven forty-five. He claimed to have been working for forty-five minutes and then left to visit his local mosque. Ian Hewson's testimony suggested someone was still in the shop after nine o'clock. As the questioning continued, Tekin suddenly lost his temper, grabbed the weapon from his coat pocket, and stabbed DI Hickerton in the upper chest. The crime scene photos from that attack show the wounds incurred by the detective were identical to those suffered by Ms Mallinder. The original images were already in evidence. When DS Latimer asked about the weapon, the defendant nodded towards DI Hickerton, who was being carried downstairs to the ambulance by paramedics. DS Latimer asked the defendant if he was saying the weapon in DI Hickerton's chest was the one he used to stab Laura Mallinder. The defendant nodded, saying it wasn't a knife. It was half a pair of scissors. An item he carried with him always."

Gus watched as Robin Burchell turned to the jury.

"My client misunderstood the question. He thought he was agreeing that he owned the half-pair of scissors in DI Hickerton. But, as I said earlier, the police cannot prove he had the murder weapon in June 2011. It had gone missing months before the murder. My client suspected which staff member might have mistakenly picked it up. However, that man has since returned to Cyprus. The police conducted forensic tests and found my client's fingerprints on the handle of the item you've just seen. But they would. After all, my client admits he was carrying it on the eighth of May. It was where it always was, in the breast pocket of the maroon jacket he wore over his street clothes every day of the week. He discovered it, hidden at the back of a drawer five or six years ago."

"My learned friend wants the jury to believe the murder weapon was in another person's possession for perhaps two years," said Ivor Kendrick. "If the defendant had treasured this item as much as he claimed, surely he would have made greater efforts to find it."

"My learned friend has missed the vital point, my lord," said Robin Burchell. "When my client had this item in his possession in 1991, it was part of a complete pair of scissors. After they broke, he kept one half as a souvenir. He says he discarded the other half in a drawer at the shop. During his time on remand, he realised the item he used to stab DI Hickerton must have been the other half. The one he discarded."

"Did the police find the other half of the pair of scissors?" asked James Denmark QC.

"No, my lord," said Kendrick.

"Then I think we'll adjourn for the day," said the judge. "Perhaps you can take advantage of the free time to get your act together."

After James Denmark swept from the room, the jury was taken out, and the gallery cleared. Gus followed Alex and Neil downstairs to the foyer. Neil went straight to the vending machines to grab a Mars bar.

"What does that mean, guv?" asked Alex. "Tekin never denied entering the parlour and trying it on with Laura. He said she laughed at him."

"Theo Hickerton was taken out of the firing line after that stabbing," said Gus. "We haven't been in touch with whoever at Gablecross progressed the investigation after we handed it over. I expect Kendrick to call Jake Latimer or his superior to the witness box in the morning to describe their subsequent interviews with Tekin. That should get the prosecution case back on track."

"It didn't help that Kendrick paraded Exhibit A in front of the jury," said Neil, still munching his chocolate bar. "They can't unsee that, can they? He made a big thing out of the unusual weapon, and the shape of the wounds was identical as made no odds from both attacks. Everyone on that jury would accept that Tekin used that weapon on Hickerton *and* Laura Mallinder."

"Tekin is claiming the item he found, hidden at the back of the drawer, was the half he'd discarded," said Gus. "I'd defy anyone to tell the difference between the two halves if they were presented to you in isolation. So, unless he admitted stabbing Laura, the defence might argue that unless the prosecution can prove the two attacks were committed with Exhibit A, someone else could have entered the parlour that night and stabbed Laura."

"Nobody else had a motive," said Alex. "Also, the window of opportunity would be smaller than ever. We know what time Maggie Monk arrived."

"Jake Latimer needs to chase down that barber who returned home to Cyprus," said Neil.

"Even if he denies ever touching anything belonging to his boss, it won't change things," said Gus.

"Because the verdict needs to be beyond a reasonable doubt," said Alex, nodding. "The defence could manage to get Exhibit A thrown out and argue the police don't have a murder weapon, and although Tekin admitted arguing with Laura, he denies killing her. That's why we're here today."

"Do you want me to run you back to Chippenham, Alex?" asked Neil.

Alex looked at his watch.

"Please. Lydia won't finish work until five."

Gus, Alex, and Neil walked outside the Crown Court building and headed for Prince's Street.

"Not how we imagined the day would go, guv," said Alex.

"Quite," said Gus.

They took the M4 to Chippenham, and after dropping Alex off at home, they drove to the bungalow.

"Same time in the morning, guv," said Neil.

"That suits me," said Gus. "Call if I need to drive myself there."

"You never know, guv," said Neil.

Neil executed a passable three-point turn in the driveway before heading home, and Gus let himself inside the bungalow. Like Alex, he was resigned to waiting a couple of hours for his better half. Gus sat in the lounge and wondered why life couldn't be straightforward.

Suzie found Gus still sitting, in the dark, when she came through the door at half-past five.

"You must have had an early finish," she said. "Did your killer see sense and plead guilty after all?"

"Far from it," said Gus. He told Suzie how the day had unfolded.

"Crikey, what a mess," said Suzie. "Surely, someone asked Tekin outright whether he'd killed Laura before he was remanded into custody?"

"We hadn't heard a whisper that Tekin was about to plead not guilty until Kenneth broke the news to me on Monday," said Gus. "We've met with Jake Chalmers at Gablecross numerous times during our other cases, and he's never said a word. That goes for Gareth Francis too, when I've bumped into him. But, because Tekin stabbed Theo Hickerton with a weapon that matched the wounds on Laura's body, it sounds like someone assumed that was proof positive they had their man."

"I can't see who else had the means, motive, and opportunity," said Suzie.

"There isn't anyone," said Gus. "But police never found the other half of the pair of scissors. If they had, it would have been game over. Jake Chalmers looked ashen when the judge suggested the prosecution gets their act together tomorrow. My guess is Jake's searching the storage facility for boxes relating to the case. Maybe it's among items removed from the barber shop, and nobody realised its significance. We'll look like mugs if that's the case, but we'd be in a better position than we are currently."

"Perhaps the defence counsel was right, and it was never there once this anonymous colleague returned to Cyprus," said Suzie.

"Why would that chap pick it up, anyway?" asked Gus. "It was useless for their job, and he had no sentimental attachment to it, unlike Tekin."

"I've seen the photographs, and Laura was an attractive young woman," said Suzie. "It's possible one of Tekin's colleagues fancied her too. Did Gablecross interview everyone working in the shop back in 2011?"

"Pass," said Gus. "It wasn't our baby. We pointed them towards Tekin as the culprit, and once he'd shown what a temper he had, lashing out at Theo Hickerton left them to join the dots."

"I hope things go better tomorrow," said Suzie. "I'm off for my shower now, and then I'll choose between the two dresses that still fit me to wear tonight."

"After the day I've had, a quiet night with friends is what I need tonight," said Gus.

He took his turn in the shower later and threw his shirt into the back of the wardrobe. When Suzie criticised anything he wore, it was best to reduce it to the role of something to be worn to the allotment; or when he was painting and decorating. Otherwise, it disappeared into one of those clothing bags stuffed through the letterbox from mysterious charities.

They donned their thick overcoats and scarves at five to eight and strolled arm-in-arm along the lane to the Lamb. Once inside, the warmth of the open fire hit them like a brick wall.

"Now that's what I call a warm welcome," said Gus. "I'm not sure I want to sit at a table too close to the hearth, though."

Suzie went to find a table, and Gus looked for the land-lord. The young woman behind the bar told him he was upstairs and wouldn't be down until ten.

Gus ordered drinks for him and Suzie and carried them towards the blazing log fire.

"Over here, Gus," she called.

Suzie was in the corner of the room, away from the direct heat but close enough to still get the benefit.

"Well done," he said. "It's not too busy yet. We'll need to book a table next Wednesday and beyond with Christmas approaching. I was hoping to have a word with the landlord. He was concerned about Bert, but one of his staff told me he'll be about later."

The rear door of the pub opened, and Clemency Bentham swept into the room, closely followed by Brett Penman. Gus felt a cold draught biting at his ankles before Brett closed the door firmly behind him.

"Those rosy cheeks suggest you two cycled here tonight," said Suzie. "How could you when it's freezing cold?"

"Call this cold?" laughed Brett. "I've known summer days this temperature back home."

Clemency sat down opposite Suzie.

"It's toasty in here," said Clemency. "Far warmer than in the rectory. I'm afraid that central heating for churches and their ministers has always been considered a luxury. So I asked Brett if he'll get me a coffee tonight rather than an ice-cold soft drink."

"Mine's thawing out gradually," said Suzie taking a sip.

Gus had followed Brett to the bar to pay for their drinks. The young girl was pouring a pint of lager, and Gus asked Brett whether he'd spoken to Bert and Irene this week.

"We dropped in for a visit on Sunday afternoon," said Brett. "Neither of them looked chipper. Of course, they're better than they were during that bout of flu, but that's about it. Clem and I had a heart-to-heart when we returned to my place that evening. We'll tell you what we decided after we've eaten."

"The landlord was concerned he hadn't seen Bert for a few days," said Gus.

"Partly concern for the old beggar," said Brett. "And

worried his till will lose a significant amount when Bert's no longer able to make it along the lane for his customary few pints of cider. So what's on the specials board tonight? Any idea?"

"That's intriguing," said Gus. "You rarely consult the specials board as long as a sizeable steak is on the main menu. If it tickles your tastebuds, the chef has given Dover sole and moussaka new twists."

"Steak it is, then," said Brett. "Let's get back to the ladies and see if we can persuade them to make a snap decision on what they want to eat." He picked up his pint and a hot coffee and returned to the table while Gus ensured the drinks went on his tab.

It was plain that neither of the ladies was in a hurry to leave the warmth of the bar, but orders were finally selected, and after they'd eaten their main course, plus a generous helping of homemade apple pie and custard to follow, they weren't in a position to move for a while, even if they wished.

"Can I get you another round of drinks?" asked the young girl who'd spoken to Gus earlier. "I'm clearing tables and helping the boss ensure everyone has everything they need. He's behind the bar now, by the way."

"We'll have four coffees, please," said Suzie.

"Right," said Brett, "and two brandies, please."

"Is that to ward off the cold, Brett?" asked Suzie.

"He needs a bit of Dutch courage," giggled the Reverend.

"We had a long discussion on Sunday night," said Brett. "My grandfather's health is a worry, and there's no escaping the fact he's eighty-six."

"We only got engaged a few weeks ago," said the Reverend. "But we never intended to wait too long before we got married. Unfortunately, recent events have shown we can't afford to wait any longer."

"So, when are you thinking?" asked Gus. "A spring wedding or late summer?"

"We notified the Bishop on Monday morning," said the Reverend. "The twenty-eight days' notice has been duly registered. We're to be married in our village church on Christmas Eve."

# Chapter Four

"CONGRATULATIONS TO YOU BOTH," said Gus. "I'm sure you'll be happy together."

"Gosh, that doesn't give you much time to arrange everything," said Suzie. "Not that I have any experience on the matter."

"I've spoken to my Aunt Margaret in New Zealand," said Brett. "After I explained the situation, she took the sensible decision in the circumstances."

"She would want to fly home, with her husband, for the funeral, whenever that may be," said Gus. "A long flight over the Christmas period would be expensive."

"Exactly," said Brett. "They're not rolling in it, and the trip to Canada, plus the stop-over in the UK in the summer, left a hole in their savings."

The coffee and brandy arrived on a tray, and the four friends returned to the topic of the wedding arrangements.

"What about your family, Clemency?" asked Suzie.

"Do they still live in Dorchester?" asked Gus.

"Yes, they're over the moon that their only daughter is

finally tying the knot. My mother thinks Brett is perfect, and despite the short notice, she'll be ready. My father seems to recall getting married at Christmas was more common in his father's day than it is now."

"Fewer couples get married anyway," said Suzie.

"You referred to yourself as their only daughter," said Gus. "Does that mean there's a married brother, or two, somewhere?"

"Just the one brother, Richard, who's four years younger than me, " said Clemency. "He's married to Ruth, and they live in Weymouth with their twin daughters. So I've asked whether Olivia and Sophie will be my bridesmaids."

"How lovely," said Suzie. "How old are they?"

"Seven and a half," said Clemency. "Can you remember how important that 'half' was when we were that age?"

"Who's doing the honours?" asked Gus. "Will the Bishop be available at St Michael's to perform the service that day?"

"Sadly not," said Clemency. "My colleague who shares the duties between the parishes we cover has agreed to fit us into her schedule. Noon on the twenty-fourth of December is a quiet spot in her calendar. So we should be okay provided another flu bug, or worse, doesn't throw up a rash of funeral services to accommodate."

"You never run out of work, do you?" said Gus.

"Two important people are needed at the wedding," said Brett. "Gus, I hope you'll agree to be my best man?"

"No problem, Brett," said Gus. "It will be a first for me, despite my age. Nobody has asked me before."

"Olivia and Sophie will need a mature guiding hand, Suzie," said Clemency. "I'd love you, as my best friend, to be my maid of honour."

"Gosh, yes, of course," said Suzie. "How exciting."

"Right, time for this brandy," said Brett. "Fingers crossed, we will celebrate Christmas and New Year with no dark clouds on the horizon. Cheers."

Gus raised his glass.

"I'll drink to that," he said.

Five minutes later, the landlord called time, and Gus went to the bar to settle the bill.

"Bert and Irene are still under the weather," Gus told him. "Brett visited them on Sunday afternoon. We can only hope they both keep clear of any coughs and colds over the holiday period."

"I hope they get better soon. Do you want me to book you a table next Wednesday evening, Mr Freeman?"

"The four of us again, please," said Gus. "By the sound of things, Suzie and the Reverend will be discussing dresses, bouquets, and an Order of Service. A wedding has been announced."

"If they need somewhere for the reception, tell them to keep us in mind. When is it?"

"Christmas Eve, at noon," said Gus. "Are you still keen?"

"It depends on how many guests they invite, but most places will be booked solid with parties in the evening. Not many businesses have lunchtime parties these days, so we might be able to squeeze them in."

"Thanks," said Gus. "I'll drop in at the weekend with an update on numbers. I imagine it's all part of the best man's duties."

"I've done it several times," said the landlord. "The most important part is getting the groom to the church on time and keeping a tight hold of the rings."

Gus caught up with the others outside, and soon he and

Suzie were watching two red rear lights disappearing in the distance as Brett and the Reverend cycled home.

"Another sharp frost in the morning, I fancy," said Suzie.

"You need to be up early to scrape your windscreen, darling. Neil will be outside the house at eight on the dot again. After that, I'll be able to get straight into a warm car with the heater on full blast."

"You can go off people, you know," said Suzie.

### Thursday, 29 November 2018

SUZIE'S FORECAST had been on the money, and a cold, crisp morning greeted Gus when he stepped outside the door at eight, fortified with another bowl of hot porridge oats. He slipped into the passenger seat beside Neil.

"By the centre, guv, it's not getting any warmer, is it?" said Neil.

"This too shall pass, Neil," said Gus.

"Another line from Shakespeare that passed me by, guv?"

"Persian, I think, Neil. It alludes to the temporary nature of the human condition."

"Too deep for me, guv," said Neil. "Was this Persian chap pointing out that neither bad nor good times in your life last forever?"

"In a nutshell, Neil," said Gus. "Easy to say when you get a fair share of both, but this week only one bright moment stands out among a mountain of misfortune. Our friends are getting married in just over three weeks."

"Another lamb to the slaughter," said Neil.

"Let's hope that Persian chap was right and something good lies around the corner."

Neil followed yesterday's route and delivered them to the Prince's Street car park by eight forty-five.

A red Mini drove past them as they approached the Crown Court building.

"Lydia can't wait to get to Gablecross, guv," said Neil. "Perhaps she enjoys working with Raj Sengupta."

"She'll get booked for speeding if she isn't careful," said Gus. "That might slow her down."

Alex was waiting in the gallery when Gus and Neil went upstairs to Court One.

"I had a brief chat with Jake Latimer on the way in, guv," said Alex. "It doesn't look good."

The court clerk got things underway again, and Gus didn't have the chance to ask Alex what he meant. Instead, he stood, with the others, as the judge made his grand entrance. When everyone was seated, James Denmark invited Ivor Kendrick and Robin Burchell to approach the raised platform where he sat. The conversation was brief, and Gus couldn't catch more than the odd word.

Robin Burchell called Jake Latimer to the witness box, and the court clerk swore him in.

"DS Latimer, do you have your pocket notebook covering the eighth of May with you, as I asked yesterday evening?"

"I do," said Jake.

"For the jury's benefit, could you briefly summarise what it's for?"

"The majority of police officers are issued with a pocket notebook which is an official document and must be carried at all times when on duty," said Jake. "This PNB has been safely stored in case it was required for reference or used when giving evidence. We record information about an offence or incident in as much detail as possible. It helps to have the best information available at a time like this. I often use my notebook to refresh my memory when giving evidence."

"Did you refer to that notebook when giving evidence yesterday, DS Latimer?"

"Yes, sir," said Jake.

"Am I right in thinking a note should be made of any comments made by a person suspected of committing an offence, whether these comments are in response to your questions or not?"

"That's correct, sir," said Jake.

"The person should be invited to read the note and write an endorsement that the notes in the PNB were a true and accurate record of the conversation. The suspect and the officer should then sign it. Is that correct?"

"The conversation may be construed to be an interview, sir. If the suspect is unhappy with what I've written, they should indicate which details are inaccurate and sign a record of those details."

"Did the defendant read your version of the events that occurred between the time you arrived on the first floor of the premises in Broadgreen with DI Hickerton and when you left him with the custody sergeant at Gablecross?"

"He did, sir," said Jake. "But he refused to sign it."

"Did he give a reason?" asked Burchell.

"The defendant claimed he was unfamiliar with many of the words," said Jake.

"Yes, he claimed he misunderstood when you asked him

if he'd used the blade you could see in DI Hickerton's chest when he stabbed Laura Mallinder. So what procedure should be followed if someone refuses to sign the notebook?"

"I should note he'd refused to sign and get it counter-signed by the senior officer present. That would be after my boss had read my notes to the suspect again and asked if it was accurate."

"Did your senior officer sign your notebook?" asked Burchell.

"Hardly," said Jake. "He was in the hospital when I returned to Gablecross."

"You realise that means we cannot be certain your note-book accurately recorded what happened that afternoon?"

"DI Hickerton was the senior officer, sir," said Jake. "Mr Freeman was downstairs and didn't see anything. He's a retired Detective Inspector, working as a consultant, and doesn't carry a warrant card."

"A civilian, to all intents and purposes," said Burchell.

"He's a detective with a stellar reputation, sir, but his powers were restricted. The other detectives at the scene were of the same rank as myself. We hadn't expected Tekin to kick off like that, and in confusion, the counter signature got overlooked."

"I imagine you were also busy after leaving court yesterday afternoon, DS Latimer. Did you have any luck hunting down the missing half the pair of scissors?"

"Since 2011, we've gathered far more evidence than could be held at Gablecross Police station, sir. It is now held at a facility on one of the local industrial estates. I located several boxes relating to the murder of Ms Mallinder and the assault on Di Hickerton. However, there was no sign of the missing half of the pair of scissors. Therefore, the item in the plastic bag labelled Exhibit A is our only piece."

"Excellent, DS Latimer," said Robin Burchell. "What about the recorded interviews at Gablecross with the senior officer who took over from DI Hickerton?"

"I couldn't find them at the off-site facility, sir," said Jake. "But, they could have been separated from the relevant boxes during the transfer."

"Does that often happen, DS Latimer?" asked Burchell.

"No, sir, it shouldn't happen, but it does. One box looks like another, and things sometimes end up in the wrong box."

"Thank you, DS Latimer, that will be all," said Burchell. "Milord, the prosecution has had sufficient time to produce the missing half of the scissors and failed. Furthermore, the notebook procedure was not followed to the letter, and vital evidence appears to have been misfiled or mislaid. I believe these are sufficient grounds for dismissal, are they not?"

"I imagine the Crown Prosecution Service is regretting their decision to charge the defendant with murder, given the shambles I've witnessed these past two days," said the judge. "Your client has already admitted he'd stabbed DI Hickerton, and Exhibit A was the weapon used in the attack. So there would have been no point in pleading not guilty. This pantomime could have been avoided."

Gus watched as the Crown Prosecution Service representatives spoke with Ivor Kendrick. A shrug of the shoulders from the prosecution counsel suggested they had decided to throw in the towel. Gus closed his eyes and tried to block out the thought that this disaster would be at his door somehow.

James Denmark QC explained to the jury what was happening, thanked them for their patience, and told them their services would no longer be required. Gus, Alex, and Neil watched the reporters rush from the room to get their stories into print as soon as possible. Members of the public had plenty to talk about as they filed out and moved downstairs.

As Gus and his two colleagues followed them out, the bottom line was that Ahmet Tekin would be remanded in custody until scheduled to appear in these courts on a charge determined by the CPS.

"What's the charge likely to be, guv?" asked Alex.

"Grievous bodily harm," said Gus. "Tekin stabbed a police officer, intending to do him harm. He wanted to stop him from asking questions about Laura Mallinder."

"The sentencing guidelines on that could add up to life imprisonment, couldn't they, guv?" asked Alex.

"My grandmother could get GBH across the winning line," said Neil. "Tekin will spend decades in prison."

"What about the victim and her family?" asked Gus. "Did you see her brothers, Gary and Tyrone, when they left the courtroom? They felt cheated. The tariff for taking a weapon to the scene and then using it to kill someone *starts* at twenty-five years. I'm sure they would have drawn some comfort from a sentence of that length if the wheels hadn't fallen off the prosecution case."

"Sorry, guv," said Neil. "I wasn't thinking."

"That's not the worst part, Neil," said Gus. "No sentence would bring Laura back, but don't imagine for a minute Tekin will spend anywhere near as long inside as you think. The maximum term for the offence is sixteen years; a guilty plea, which he will undoubtedly enter, could reduce his sentence. So Tekin may only serve twelve years, at most."

"You weren't to blame, guv," said Alex.

"Where does that leave us now, guv?" asked Neil. "The Chief Constable thought we'd be tied up in court for a week or more."

"Let's get Alex home," said Gus. "Then, you can drop me at London Road to get an audience with the boss. I'll call both of you tonight with our next assignment."

There was little conversation on the motorway as Neil negotiated the midday traffic heading west. Then, after dropping Alex at home, they were heading for Devizes when Neil's phone rang.

"There's a lay-by two hundred yards on your left, Neil," said Gus. "I can't see a balloon, but you never know."

Neil checked his phone.

"Mother-in-law," he said. "Just wanted to let me know the central heating's on the blink."

"At her place or yours?" asked Gus.

"Our place," said Neil. "Melody was frightened of ringing me because we could do without the expense."

"It might be something simple," said Gus, more in hope than expectation.

Even the most straightforward task had central heating engineers shaking their heads and querying the number of years you said you'd had the boiler. Gus wondered whether they attended the same training courses as car mechanics.

"Here we are at HQ, guv," said Neil. Gus realised they'd arrived at London Road while he'd been daydreaming. Neil had parked by the steps to the front door of the main building.

"Thanks, Neil. I'll speak to you later," said Gus.

He signed in at Reception and headed upstairs. Vera was sitting at her desk.

"I didn't expect to see you this afternoon, Gus," she said. "What's the matter?"

"Bad news usually travels fast," said Gus. "To cut a long story short, the court case collapsed. The CPS was made to look like chumps, which they don't appreciate. I wanted to warn Kenneth they'll try shifting the blame elsewhere."

"He's alone at the moment," said Vera picking up the phone. "You go ahead. I'll call him to say you're on your way."

Gus crossed the mezzanine and was about to knock on Kenneth's door when it opened.

"Get in here, Freeman," said the Chief Constable. "What went wrong?"

Gus spent the next thirty minutes bringing Kenneth up to speed. He wasn't surprised his boss got out of his chair and walked to the window. Whatever helped Kenneth calm down was fine by him. On occasions like this, Gus was thankful architects had improved window design over the years. There was zero chance of anyone throwing themselves out of the windows in this building.

"I thought a week at Crown Court would be helpful," said Kenneth. "It would keep you out of mischief while the others were assigned differing duties."

"Best laid plans, sir," said Gus. "I was spitting feathers when I first heard the news, but I understand why the PCC needed to remedy the situation. Budget cuts have reduced your wiggle room, with several departments down to the bare bones. It only takes a flu virus, an unplanned pregnancy, or a senior officer with wandering hands, and certain vital services are under threat."

"Is there anything you don't know, Freeman?" sighed Kenneth. "Terry Davis had a spy network the envy of the CIA, but you run him close. Who told you?"

"I have to protect my sources, sir," said Gus.

"That suggests an inside job," said Kenneth. "DI Ferris must have told you the gory details."

"We're not the only ones with a problem, sir," said Gus.

"I don't want this to go further than these four walls, Freeman," said the Chief Constable. "But the Met is sitting on a mountain of complaints from the public, and serving officers, about similar offences. Some of them are a darn sight worse. The armed forces, the fire brigade and the police, have been featured in stories in the media in recent months. So which is it, Freeman? Is it the uniform that attracts a certain type of predator, or do the services I mention merely reflect the situation across the whole population?"

"I fear it's the latter, sir," said Gus.

"In that case, God help us," said Kenneth.

He returned from the window and sat down.

"I'm tired," he said. "The end of March can't come soon enough."

Kenneth's phone rang. He listened, closed his eyes, and replaced the handset.

"That was the PCC. He's on the warpath. I'm to report to him in fifteen minutes."

"I know you're busy, sir," said Gus. "Did you plan anything in case Tekin changed his mind and pleaded guilty?"

"Is DS Davis still available?" asked Kenneth.

"For the time being, sir," said Gus.

"ACC Gregory has launched a new initiative," said the Chief Constable. "We've suffered from county lines for several years and the homes of vulnerable adults being taken over by criminals. Gang kingpins who exploit children to sell their drugs can expect to be evicted from their council homes shortly. ACC Gregory and the borough council intend stronger action against the Swindon-based gang leaders. Those responsible for a growing youth gang culture on the three largest housing estates must learn their time is up. We're looking at injunctions designed to stop groups congregating as part of a clampdown on youths responsible for anti-social behaviour, drug dealing and violence."

"Swindon hasn't experienced the violent inter-gang rivalries of London, sir," said Gus. "But when we've visited Gablecross recently, we've heard stories of young people attacking each other with machetes in north Swindon. So something had to give."

"ACC Gregory has initiated a series of drug raids and installed extra patrols," said Kenneth. "Her colleague, DI Gareth Francis, works closely with the council's housing department. Council officers joined DI Francis on a raid on a Pinehurst council house last week."

"Where do DS Hardy and DS Davis fit into this initiative, sir?" asked Gus.

"While ACC Gregory has promised to take a stronger line against the gang leaders, more is being invested in early-intervention programmes aimed at diverting youngsters from a life of crime," said Kenneth. "She has two early-intervention officers based at Gablecross Police Station working full-time supporting young people. Your two sergeants would temporarily bring that number to four."

"So, it's not just a case of enforcement," said Gus. "Good, we're investing in preventing the criminal exploitation of young people and understanding how we can intervene and support them and their families."

"ACC Gregory and DI Francis make a good team," said the Chief Constable.

Gus couldn't resist a smile.

"Not again," sighed Kenneth. "What have you heard now?"

"They've been seen socialising late at night, sir," said Gus.

"Why should I worry? Sylvia Robbins can sort that out if it becomes a problem. After the successful raid in Pinehurst, the council hopes everyone in the community will take note that this kind of disruptive activity will no longer be tolerated. A small minority can't be allowed to ruin the quality of life for everyone else."

"Do you want me to inform Alex Hardy and Neil Davis they're off to Gablecross tomorrow, sir?

"If you would, Freeman. I might not have time today. Look, you'd better have this Crees and Hayward file. We can't have you sitting around without a thing to do. DI Packenham should be able to look after a handful of uniforms and PCSOs. I'll ask DC Umeh to be released from Farm Watch duties after tomorrow. You can set up a base at Bourne Hill and liaise with Crockett and Tubbs, or whatever they're called.

"Crocker and Mears, sir," said Gus. "Will DS Mercer give Bourne Hill a heads-up to warn them the Prodigal Son is about to return?"

"I've asked him to see if Bourne Hill can find a few square feet of office space for the foreseeable future," said Kenneth. "Whether Mercer's budget will stretch to a fatted calf, I have my doubts. You haven't had any issues on the occasional visit in the past months, have you?"

"Not a bit of it, sir," said Gus. "I still have good friends there, some of them I've known for decades. We've popped in for an hour because it was a convenient spot for an interview with a local. But, staying there to pick holes in a case investigated by senior members of staff sitting in a nearby office is quite another."

"Water off a duck's back to someone like you, Freeman," said the Chief Constable. "I'll ensure Mercer keeps an eye on things. Let him know at once if you or DC Umeh aren't made to feel welcome."

"Thank you, sir," said Gus. "Will that be all?"

"I need to get on," said Kenneth. "Use the rest of today and tomorrow to familiarise yourself with the case, get settled in at your old stamping-ground, and start work in earnest on Monday morning."

"Message received and understood," said Gus. He picked up the large folder and left Kenneth to prepare for his grilling from Stuart Midwinter.

Vera and Kassie were nowhere in sight when he crossed the administration floor to the stairs. Gus sat in the Focus for a few minutes deciding whether to go home first, read the file, or drive to Salisbury now to learn where he and Blessing would be working.

Gus decided an hour at the bungalow for coffee, and a snack would help clear his head of the trials and tribulations the morning in Swindon had brought. So, as he eased the Focus through the gateway, he was thankful the frosty conditions of the early morning were a distant memory.

He'd seen the van belonging to the local postie parked in the lane, but nothing was on the mat when he stepped inside. If someone up there were orchestrating his recent ominous sequence of events, a brown envelope indicating he'd been selected for jury duty would have arrived today.

While the kettle boiled, Gus checked the boiler had turned on and off at the prescribed times. After hearing of Neil's woes, it reminded Gus he tended to take these things for granted. When he and Tess moved to the bungalow, they'd had a new boiler, extra radiators, and a range of white goods installed and foolishly assumed they wouldn't need to worry about them for twenty years.

Gus was satisfied nothing needed replacing before the baby was due and returned to the kitchen. He made a sandwich and flicked through the case folder as he ate. Kenneth's highlights page rekindled Gus's memories from his younger days in Salisbury.

John Crees and Amanda Howard had lived on Rampart Road, just a four-minute drive from the police station. These days, Gus noticed that he and Blessing could walk to the terraced property in six. The old city had changed so much since he was a young boy. The present police station overlooked where the A36 and A30 converged close to the city centre.

Gus had lived with his parents on Laverstock Road, which wasn't much further from the station than Rampart Road, just half a mile to the northeast. He could remember making a regular five-minute cycle ride to watch the progress on the new ring road during the school holidays.

Everybody knew the ring road was going to happen, but when it did, Gus didn't think his parents ever went close enough to look at it to see what was going on. Of course, they knew what was there before: a lovely road – two or three roads leading to the London Road. During Gus's early teens, traffic was always solid from the market on August Bank Holidays. There was a desperate need for the new road, but when it arrived, it scarred the Greencroft. That park was the green lung of the Milford Street bridge area. It provided grassy recreation space and a play area for younger children, and many magnificent trees were planted in 1897 to mark Queen Victoria's Diamond Jubilee. Today's Greencroft was bordered on three sides by the ring road,

Bourne Hill and Greencroft Street, but it used to cover a much larger area before the Ring Road cut a swathe through it. All those memories crowded into Gus's head as he skimmed those first few pages of the murder file.

John Crees had moved into the house on Rampart Road with Mandy Howard in the autumn of 2010. Neighbours described them as a devoted couple, very outgoing, and involved in the local biking community. John had struggled to find work after leaving the Army and found himself in Salisbury at the turn of the century, taking general labouring jobs to make ends meet.

Mandy Howard had moved to Salisbury from Merthyr Tydfil, a town in the valleys, twenty miles north of the Welsh capital, Cardiff, in the summer of 2009. She worked for the local council as an administration assistant during the day and three evenings a week behind the bar of the Winchester Gate, a pub not a stone's throw from their front door.

John finished work at five on Friday, the nineteenth of October in 2012 and told his boss, Mike Woodman, he would see him at seven-thirty on Monday morning. They were due to drive to Old Sarum on the edge of the Plain to start the groundwork on a plot of land bought for development. That day was the first step towards five four-bedroomed luxury properties to strengthen Mike's pension fund.

John collected Mandy from The Winchester Gate at midnight on Saturday evening, and they walked home along Rampart Road.

That was the last time anyone recalled seeing either of them alive, except for their killer.

Mike Woodman stopped his van by the junction of Wessex Road and Wain-along-Road at seven-thirty on

Monday. John wasn't leaning against the wall in his usual position. Mike called John's mobile but got no reply. Mike couldn't afford to hang around, so he called another labourer who had retired from his firm six months earlier and offered him a day's work.

After returning from Old Sarum on Monday evening, Mike tried John's number again. Still, there was no reply. So at seven o'clock, he drove to Rampart Road to see what had happened to him. John had been such a reliable soul throughout the time they'd worked together that it seemed totally out of character.

Mike rang the front door bell. The curtains upstairs and downstairs were closed, which wasn't unusual at that time of night in October, but he could see no lights on inside. So, Mike walked up the alleyway at the end of the row of terraced properties and checked for lights or movement.

Again, there was nothing obviously wrong. Mike stood and thought for a bit. What could have happened? Perhaps, there'd been a family emergency in South Wales, and John and Mandy had driven across the Severn Bridge in a rush, forgetting to notify him. That didn't feel like John's style. At the very least, he would have sent Mike a text apologising for letting him down and promising to return to work as soon as they had averted the crisis.

Mike tried the back gate. It wasn't locked, so he walked up the garden path and approached the back door. A window pane in the back door was broken. Mike put his shoulder on the door and forced his way inside. He called out for John and Mandy by name, but the house was dark and eerily quiet. Once Mike had checked they weren't in the rooms on the ground floor, he climbed the stairs. His dread of what he might find grew with every tread.

When he turned on the light in the front bedroom, Mike

found them lying on their blood-soaked bed. John appeared to have been trying to protect Mandy with his body. Both had been battered around the head so severely that their heads had effectively been destroyed.

Mike raced downstairs, ran outside, and vomited into the flower bed by the neighbour's fence. Still shaking, he dialled 999.

# Chapter Five

GUS CHECKED the police surgeon's initial comments and closed the file. That was more than enough for a first glance. If nobody saw the couple after they left the Winchester Gate on Saturday, then it was clear from Jeff Sheppard's report that the attack occurred after they'd fallen asleep that night.

Jeff had been one of the local GPs on-call at Bourne Hill when Gus worked there. Jeff would be in his seventies now if memory served, but Gus thought he would have heard a whisper from his former colleagues if he'd died.

Gus tidied the kitchen before he left and drove to Salisbury with the Crees and Hayward file beside him on the passenger seat. He hoped his lunch break had given Geoff Mercer time to pave the way for his arrival.

Forty minutes after leaving the bungalow, Gus had parked in the visitor's car park at Bourne Hill. He approached the Reception desk, hoping to see a friendly face. DS Bob Martin filled the bill.

"Afternoon, Gus," said Bob. "Nice day for it. I hear you're moving back in."

"Good to see you, Bob," said Gus. "I don't wish to impose on your nick's legendary hospitality any longer than necessary. I'm enjoying the freedom my usual office gives me."

"The rumour is the Commissioner is behind this temporary transfer," said Bob. "Of course, we get news third-hand at best out here on the edge of the county, so that I could be wrong."

"The PCC said he was keen to utilise the other members of my team in a way he felt was best," said Gus. "My views on the matter didn't hold much weight. I'm sure you suffer the same treatment. Despite forty years of loyal service under your belt, they feel it's acceptable to move you around at a minute's notice."

"I think it's time I spoke with my superiors," sighed Bob. "These buildings are already being shared with people from the Council. No doubt they'll finally decide where we're going next. It's been on the cards for a while. I had plenty of happy days here, and they'll never return."

"Ah, the good old days," said Gus. "You don't wear glasses, Bob. So it must be the rose-tinted contact lenses."

"Come on, Gus," said Bob. "The job has changed that much I don't recognise it. It would help if you were young and prepared to bend with the wind to fit in these days. I'm frightened to say something that will get me sacked without a pension. How do you avoid the pitfalls, Gus? You were never afraid to say what you thought."

"I'm thankful for the diverse, young team Geoff Mercer gave me, Bob," said Gus. "I'm learning from them every day. Although, I'll admit to teaching them some of my old methods, too, hoping they don't complain. So far, a mix of the old and new has yielded positive results. Whether we achieve the same on our latest case remains to be seen."

"Trust you, Gus Freeman," said Bob shaking his head. "You never change. Please don't ask me. They keep me in the dark about what's going on. All I heard was you would be in an office close to Phil Crocker."

"Interesting," said Gus. "Perhaps he wants us close enough to keep an eye on. We're taking a fresh look at one of his old cases. Do you remember when Spider Crees and his partner died?"

"That was a tough one to forget for those that worked the case," said Bob. "Whoever those two bikers upset did a number on them. Forensics didn't recover a weapon at the scene, but the best guess was the killer used a four-pound lump hammer."

"Did that guess come from the paper suit brigade, or did Dr Sheppard come to that conclusion after the autopsy? Is Jeff Sheppard still around?"

"He retired about two years after that murder, at the end of 2014," said Bob. "The wife and I went to the party they held. We'd been on his list at the surgery for three decades. The young girl we've got now tries her best, but it's not the same."

"Can I find Jeff in Salisbury?" asked Gus. "I'd like to catch up with him and discuss the case."

"He's moved into a care home recently, but I've got Jeff's new address at home," said Bob. "I've got your mobile number somewhere. You asked me to keep in touch about Tony Brown, if you recall."

Gus nodded. Another former colleague, Tony Brown, passed soon after Gus had spoken to him about the Ian McGuire shooting.

"Send me the details when you've got a minute, Bob," said Gus. "Right, where do I find DI Crocker?"

"DCI Crocker these days, believe it or not," said Bob. He leaned forward to whisper the next bit. "Phil's another of those officers that need promoting to a point where he can't do any real damage if you get my drift."

"I do," said Gus. "You were closer to the action back in 2012. Did you get the feeling something was lacking in the investigation?"

"Apart from witnesses and forensic evidence, d'you mean?" asked Bob. "They couldn't make much headway with the few scraps they gathered, but once the intimidation started, the case lost its way and soon got wrapped up."

"Fair enough," said Gus. "I've only skimmed through a few highlights so far. It's too soon to judge whether Crocker and Mears did a decent job."

Bob told him where to find DCI Crocker, and it didn't take Gus long to find him. Phil Crocker's office was only twelve feet from the spot Gus had called home for many years. Of course, there had been alterations to the layout since he left, but the windows hadn't moved. Four-foot high partitions had replaced floor-to-ceiling stud walls and a door.

The current resident of the cubicle was a care-worn-looking individual in his fifties who barely moved when Gus reached his large desk.

"Good morning, sir," said Gus. "Gus Freeman. You were expecting me."

Phil Crocker studied Gus, and then his eyes moved to the large folder under his left arm.

"DS Mercer called. I've moved a DI from the work station two doors down. I thought it might bring back memories. So, I suppose you will tell me and Bob Mears where we went wrong?"

"I'd like to hear what isn't necessarily in the murder file, sir," said Gus. "That will only give me facts and figures. I need feelings, impressions, and ideas you and DS Mears had six years ago but weren't thought worth pursuing. Or which had to be abandoned when your bosses decided you'd spent long enough on the case. I sense you believe I've been sent here on a witch hunt. Nothing could be further from the truth. First, I'm here for Spider Crees and Mandy Howard. Second, I'm here because their families deserve to know who killed them and why. If there is a third reason, then if there was something to be learned about handling a murder case such as that one, we'll add it to the force's collective knowledge to help detectives in the future. I know only too well that serving officers like yourself have to do more, better, with less every day, sir. Pointing fingers and attaching blame isn't going to help any of us achieve that goal, is it?"

DCI Crocker didn't reply. Instead, he merely nodded towards the work station where Gus and Blessing would work.

Gus looked around the large open-plan office. There were far more computers, screens, and whiteboards than when he was here last and fewer bodies. They could have been former colleagues, but the partitions only gave him the tops of several heads to go on.

The desk the unnamed Detective Inspector abandoned was equipped with little that Gus and Blessing would need. It wasn't the warmest of welcomes, but they wouldn't spend much time in the cubicle. The answers lay outside, somewhere in the city streets.

Gus sat at the desk and reopened the murder file.

The first sheet of paper he came across featured a

photocopy of a newspaper article with a photograph of DI Crocker outside the house on Rampart Road. A couple in their thirties were bludgeoned to death in their own home, and a Salisbury detective described it as one of the most vicious killings he'd ever encountered. John Crees, thirty-nine, and Amanda Howard, thirty-six, had lived together on Rampart Road for two years.

Behind that sheet of paper was a quote from Dr Jeffery Sheppard, the local GP, who was interviewed after the inquest. He said the couple's way of life may not have appealed to those from a more conventional background, but they appeared to be perfectly harmless and innocent people who worked for a living and were in a stable relationship. Nevertheless, if anyone knew or suspected who was responsible for the savage murders, they should come forward.

That fell on stony ground, thought Gus. He continued to study the file until half-past four and then checked whether there was anywhere he could leave the folder in a secure place. Phil Crocker's space was empty, so Gus decided to take it home. In the morning, he'd ask the DCI for a lockable filing cabinet, plus every available key.

Gus made his way back to the main entrance. Bob Martin was deep in conversation with a member of the public but gave a friendly wave. Gus acknowledged him and walked outside to the Focus. The return journey took a little longer, but that was to be expected—a dark night, rush hour traffic, and traffic lights interrupted the flow.

When Gus arrived at twenty-five past five, Suzie wasn't home, so he parked the Focus under the neatly trimmed rambling roses and went indoors. Gus went to the kitchen to start cooking their evening meal. He soon heard the familiar bark of the Golf as it made its final spurt from the gateway to its usual resting place.

"Vera tells me you've had one of those days, darling."

Suzie kicked off her shoes and hung her winter coat in the hallway.

She joined Gus in the kitchen, stood behind him, and wrapped her arms around him.

"Notice anything?" she asked.

"You can't get as close to me as you could?" said Gus.

"Stand perfectly still," said Suzie. "There, did you feel that?"

"A kick," said Gus," and now another one. That makes life more bearable."

"The little devil started his Zumba workout while I accelerated away from London Road in a rush to get home to see you," said Suzie.

"Do you want me to stop making dinner?" asked Gus.

"No, you carry on. I'll have a shower and get changed. You can fill in the gaps that Vera wasn't privy to, and I'll tell you the latest from London Road."

By six-thirty, they'd eaten, loaded the dishwasher, made coffee, and sat on a settee in the lounge.

"Right," said Suzie. "You go first."

"My first job is to call Alex and Neil," said Gus.

He called Alex, and after listening to Lydia moaning about Raj Sengupta for two minutes, he spoke to Alex and passed the message from the Chief Constable that he and Neil had been seconded to Gablecross until Christmas. They were to report to Gareth Francis at nine in the morning.

"I've attended the courses, guv," said Alex. "Not sure about Neil. Early intervention supports youngsters at risk of poor outcomes and tackling the problems they face before they become worse. It could be a school-based programme to improve social and emotional skills or mentoring schemes for young people vulnerable to involvement in crime."

"ACC Gregory is behind the initiative," said Gus. "She reckons that, for the time being, organised crime is a bigger threat to the UK than terrorism, and it's important to intervene before it's too late."

"I'll let Lydia speak to you, guv," said Alex. "She misses the office banter."

"Early intervention not only helps the children but the community as a whole," said Lydia. "A project in Glasgow saved more than half a million pounds for Glasgow City Council over six months. After receiving support, only ten percent of the young people involved continued to offend."

"Children don't choose their childhood," said Gus, "but we can choose to help."

"I wish I'd been chosen to work with Neil and Alex on this one, guv," said Lydia. "It's a chance to make a difference. Rather like when we're working with you."

"It's only temporary, Lydia," said Gus. "If it's any consolation, you wouldn't have been happy with the office accommodation in Salisbury. Blessing and I will be working in a shoe box. Anyway, I need to call Neil. Make a note on your social calendar for next Friday, the seventh of December. We're having a team night at the Waggon & Horses."

"Terrific," said Lydia. "Thanks, guv."

Gus ended the call and rang Neil.

"Still here, guv," said Neil, "and the central heating is working now thank goodness. My next-door neighbour had a look, got it going again, and told me to pray it keeps running until Sunday when he'll have time to do a full service. Mother-in-law is still moaning that it's too cold to bring a new-born home to, but if she keeps talking, the hot air should keep the rest of us warm. Sorry, guv, did you want something?"

Gus told Neil where he needed to be tomorrow.

"Alex and Lydia will travel to Gablecross together, so you need to make your own way there,"

"Got it, guv," said Neil.

Before ending the call, Gus told Neil about the night out at the Waggon & Horses.

"I'll make it if I can, guv," said Neil. "We can combine the team night out with wetting the baby's head."

"Best wishes from Suzie and me, Neil," said Gus. "Goodnight."

"Right, now let's hear what happened today," said Suzie.

Gus went through the morning's events at the Crown Court and his visit to London Road to warn Kenneth Truelove the CPS were on the warpath.

"Nobody can blame you, or the team, Gus," said Suzie. "The CPS chose to put all their eggs in one basket. So, what did you do after you spoke to Kenneth?"

"I came here for lunch, read the case highlights, and then drove to Bourne Hill to settle in."

"How did that go?" asked Suzie.

"I don't think DCI Crocker is keen on us digging up the past," said Gus. "Bob Martin gave me a warm welcome. Those were the only two people I spoke to, so I'll reserve judgement. I can't say mixing it with the local biker community fills me with any joy, so I'll start looking else-where for answers. Tomorrow, I hope to set up meetings with the police surgeon, the landlord at the Winchester Gate pub, and Mike Woodman, the chap who employed John Crees. Mandy Howard worked for the Council, so some of her former colleagues might even be working at

Bourne Hill. All in all, I shouldn't need to spend too long in the office."

"The shoe box," said Suzie.

"It's not that bad," said Gus. "I said that to make Lydia feel better."

"You're all heart," said Suzie. "Do you want to talk about the case tonight?"

"I feel I've only scratched the surface," said Gus. "Plenty of time for you to analyse my progress, and offer words of wisdom, this time next week."

"I'll make a date in my diary," said Suzie.

"You were going to tell me about the latest news from London Road," said Gus.

"Portishead, actually," said Suzie. "I heard the news just before I left to drive home. DI Wallis resigned rather than face the charges to be laid against him at the hearing."

"That means he goes on the advisory list and will remain on that list for five years," said Gus. "DI Wallis was under investigation for gross misconduct, which could have led to dismissal. But, instead, his victims didn't get their chance to see him face-to-face because it was a closed meeting, and now there won't be any urgent necessity for a report to be published."

"Typical," said Suzie. "Officers found guilty and dismissed are placed on a barred list. Police forces and other policing bodies must refer to that list before making appointments. They're prohibited by law from employing anyone on the barred list. Can Wallis apply to have his name removed from the advisory list?"

"He could, after five years," said Gus. "But Wallis's age alone would count against him by then if he was thinking of rejoining in some capacity. The investigator will indicate in their report whether there was evidence a criminal offence had been committed. That will get passed up the chain of command for someone to decide whether the matter should be formally referred to the CPS. If they did, the CPS could still decide whether to bring charges against DI Wallis."

"So, there's still a chance he won't get away with it scot-free," said Suzie. "Not exactly a great result for the young women who have suffered, though, is it?"

"Kenneth and I had a similar conversation earlier," said Gus. "It's clear we have a lot to do."

### Friday, 30 November 2018

GUS WAS first out of bed in the morning. He needed to leave ten minutes before Suzie to give a good impression. Phil Crocker would be the first to moan if he strolled in at a quarter past nine. Although serving officers could never determine when their day would start or finish, those civilians employed for the hackneyed nine-to-five shift were expected to toe the line.

Suzie found Gus in the kitchen preparing breakfast when she surfaced.

"Will you be late tonight?" she asked with a yawn.

"Heavens, no," said Gus. "If I can leave Bourne Hill at five on the dot, I should be home soon after you. It's your turn to cook, anyway. Or was there something else you had in mind?"

"I'd like to finish the weekly shop tonight and visit my parents tomorrow morning. Since I stopped riding, we haven't seen them for a while, and it will give me a chance to catch up with Grace and Blessing."

"We should wait until mid-morning," said Gus. "Jackie's two lodgers will enjoy a lie-in and brunch on a Saturday. It would be churlish of us to interrupt that."

"I suppose you'll want to get back to Urchfont to work on the allotment," said Suzie.

"Another two hours of winter digging will break the back of it," said Gus. "As long as we're back from Worton by one o'clock, I'll be okay."

Gus and Suzie tucked into breakfast, and Gus was ready to leave the house by twenty-past eight.

"Wrap up warm, sweetheart," said Gus as he stepped through the front door. "It's a chill wind out here."

As Gus walked to the car, he thought November was making sure it had left its mark. One year it's all wind, rain, and fog; the next, it's bright and dry, but temperatures stubbornly refuse to reach double figures. Gus was thankful for the heater in the Focus as he set off along the lane. The dashboard clock read eight fifty-eight when he switched off the engine in the visitor's car park at Bourne Hill.

There was no delay at Reception today, and Bob Martin quickly handed him a lanyard.

"Everyone who remembers you from before knows you're back, Gus," said Bob. "But this ID will let the newbies know it's not Bring Your Grandfather To Work Day."

"Every joke a winner, Bob," said Gus. "Is DS Mears about this morning?"

"You'll find him on the opposite side of the room from Phil Crocker," said Bob. "You can't miss Mears's desk. It's hidden under hundreds of files and pictures of his prize lurchers."

Gus went upstairs to his workstation and dropped the case folder on his desk, which only carried a sheen of dust.

"Shaking things up as usual," said a voice as Gus waved a hand to clear the air.

Gus looked over his shoulder to see Bob Mears grinning by the doorway.

"Hello, Bob," said Gus. "You saved me a trip. Can you spare me an hour to run through the John Crees and Amanda Howard case today or Monday? The Chief Constable has asked me to take a fresh look. To see if we can't bring closure for the family."

"DCI Crocker filled me in," said Mears. "He's not a happy chappy."

"I can't see why," said Gus. "Every murder case which doesn't produce a result gets a regular review. It's how we make a better fist of the next murder investigation the first time around. What happened to you, Bob? How come you're still a DS? You and Phil made a decent team, as I remember."

"I think that was part of my problem," said Mears. "I was a good number two and not ambitious, unlike my gaffer. So, Phil moved up the ladder, and I've been teamed up with a succession of Detective Inspectors who wouldn't be without me. At least, for a year or so, until they transfer to another county, or the Met, leaving me behind."

"It's not too late, Bob," said Gus. "Shoot for the moon. You'll regret it if you don't. What about this get-together, then? When can it be?"

"I can pop back at eleven. Will that do?" said Mears.

"That'll be fine," said Gus. "I'll work my other appointments around that. See you at eleven."

Bob Mears set off for his spot on the other side of the office.

"One more thing, Bob," called Gus. "Which Council departments have employees working in these buildings?

Amanda Howard worked for the Council from 2009 to 2012, right? I want to talk to people who knew her."

"They don't bother us, so we don't bother them," said Mears. "Didn't you see the signs outside? Housing, planning, adult care, and the registrars all work here, plus you can complain about a neighbour playing reggae music all night."

"Got it," said Gus.

"There should be details of the interviews we had with her colleagues in those files on your desk," said Mears. "They weren't much help. A motive for the savage killing was elusive. Amanda never had any disagreements or arguments with anybody. As far as her work colleagues were concerned, nobody bore her a long-standing grudge."

"What about her family back in Wales?" asked Gus. "Look, forget it, for now. We'll pick it up again in a couple of hours."

Bob Mears crossed the office to his desk, and Gus went downstairs to check which of those departments Bob had mentioned might need an administration assistant. Somehow, it didn't fit the imaginative titles they preferred in the modern world.

When he was standing outside studying the signage, Gus wished he hadn't draped his coat over the back of his chair. It was parky out here with just a jacket on. Which departments might generate the most bile from the council's residents? Bob Mears reckoned Mandy Howard didn't have an enemy in the world, but Gus had been caught out too often by assuming a female victim just happened to be in the wrong place at the wrong time with a male partner. Was it possible the answer lay in the Welsh valleys? Could Mandy have been in a toxic relationship in Merthyr Tydfil? Had she escaped to Salisbury until her husband or boyfriend tracked her down?

Gus decided it was too cold to stand around, hoping the signs would provide an answer. So instead, he decided to fetch his coat from inside and check the murder file for Mike Woodman's contact details.

"Woodman and Son. How can I help you?"

The voice sounded too young for the man who had employed John Crees.

"Mike Woodman?" asked Gus.

"It is. Did you want to speak to my father?"

Gus made a mental note. If he and Suzie were blessed with a son, he would resist the temptation to name him Augustus. Unfortunately, it showed a lack of imagination, which led to confusion, as evidenced by this phone call.

"I'd like to meet with him if possible," said Gus. "My name's Freeman, a consultant working for Wiltshire Police. Your father employed John Crees for several years, so I need to speak with him."

"I remember," said Mike Junior. "Mr Crees was killed with his partner in Rampart Road about six years ago. Dad's off work with a bad back at present. I'm hoping he'll be back at work in the New Year. You'll find him at home, being fussed over by my mother."

"Do you still live at the same address?" asked Gus.

"I guess you've got the details from the original investigation," said Mike Junior. "I was in my last year at school when that murder occurred. Mum reckoned she lost count of the times Dad suffered nightmares after finding the bodies as he did."

"It's never pleasant," said Gus. "I found the address in the file before I rang you. Salisbury was my old stamping-ground, so I know I can walk to the address in ten minutes from Bourne Hill. Could you tell your mother I'm on my way?"

"Sure, Mr Freeman," said Mike Junior. "Shall I ask her to put the kettle on?"

"You've been watching too many TV shows, young man," said Gus. "But I wouldn't say no to a black coffee."

Gus ended the call and grabbed his overcoat. Wessex Road was home to modest three-bedroomed semi-detached properties which had been there from the beginning of the 1930s. Gus remembered them as being a step-up from what his parents could afford. Perhaps Woodman and Son hadn't profited from that expensive housing development in the pipeline when John Crees had been killed. Or maybe, Mike Senior did not flaunt his good fortune with a monster truck on the driveway of a super-extended family home.

As he set off from Bourne Hill Police Station, the memories flooded back. Two minutes later, Gus realised he had reached the spot where he'd stood, dumbfounded, holding his little red-and-white bicycle all those years ago. The main thing Gus could remember was seeing the aftermath of all those houses being knocked down. They had disappeared in no time, and suddenly he'd arrived one sunny afternoon and found part of the town was cut off.

There were barriers everywhere. He couldn't get to Rampart Road or Milford Street, and the air was filled with dust, dirt, and chalk from the bulldozers and diggers. It had taken some time before his teenage mind could visualise what the new road would look like when finished. Now, people living on Rampart Road had an elevated section of the A36 not forty feet from their front door. Along the London Road, to his left, Gus remembered that opposite Estcourt Road, there had been four bungalows, nice bungalows too, that were set back from the road. On her way back from the shops, his mother often walked past those bunga-lows, and Gus had asked if someone she knew lived there.

"Just daydreaming, Gus," she would say.

Gus realised people were staring at him, standing on a traffic island in the middle of a street that hadn't been there when he was barely seventeen.

Gus shrugged his shoulders against the cold and set off for Wessex Road.

He'd visited Salisbury on several occasions since he'd retired but never felt the emotional pull he was experiencing today. So perhaps it was a mistake to set up base at Bourne Hill? He was sure those gathering clouds signalled danger in one form or another, but in what direction was it coming?

# Chapter Six

GUS ARRIVED at the address on Wessex Road after a stroll down Memory lane. No monster trucks were on the driveway, just a three-year-old Renault Clio, which suggested Mrs Woodman was home. Gus rang the front doorbell and waited for the lady of the house.

"I wondered whether it was you," she said when she opened the door. "My son rang to say a Mr Freeman wanted to speak to Mike, but I thought it couldn't be. I was sure I read in the Journal that you retired a few years back. I was so sorry to hear about Tess."

Gus tried to place the face.

"It's Sally. I used to work with Tess when you two first met. I was Sally Hale back then."

"Of course, I remember you now," said Gus. "It's a small world. How's your husband today? Is he up for a guest?"

Sally grimaced and stood back to let Gus into the hallway to escape the biting wind.

"I could never fault Mike's work ethic," she sighed as

she shut the door. "But after the best part of forty years of back-breaking graft, he's got a job to stand up straight some days. This is the third or fourth time in the last three years Mike's been laid up with a bad back. It will ease enough eventually for Mike to get back out there with Micky. He can't afford to retire, or that's what he keeps telling me."

Sally Woodman opened the door to the lounge.

"Mike. Gus Freeman's here. I'll bring your coffee through in a tick. Black, without, wasn't it, Gus?"

"As ever, Sally. Thanks," said Gus.

Mike Woodman was sitting in the corner of a settee, propped up by several cushions. He looked comfortable enough until he tried to move. Gus could see the pain etched into the lines on his face.

"Don't try to get up on my account, Mike," said Gus. "I hadn't realised I would bump into a familiar face, but I first met your wife over forty years ago. Sally would have been twentyish, I suppose."

"Sally's three years older than me," said Mike. "I'm fifty-eight in years, but going on eighty-five based on the state of my body. Did you two live on the same estate in Salisbury?"

"No, my parents lived on Laverstock Road," said Gus. "I went to school in the city, and although my parents were keen I continued my studies, I always knew what I wanted to do. I joined the police in 1975, and Amesbury was my first posting after I completed training. I got plenty of variety on the beat in a rural town like Amesbury, but two years later, I transferred to my home town."

"Were you still living at home?" asked Mike.

The door opened, and Sally brought in two cups of coffee and placed a plate of biscuits next to Gus.

"Mike's not allowed," she cautioned. "But don't hold

back. I remember Tess telling me you were partial to a biscuit."

"I won't say no to a Bourbon," said Gus. "Yes, Mike, I was still single and living at home. One of the uniformed sergeants urged me to take my sergeant's exams. I saw an advert on the notice board at Bourne Hill, and I joined the detective squad in February 1978. Tess and I met in The Swan at Stoford six months later. I was having a beer with mates one evening when Tess arrived with a group of teachers celebrating the end of the summer term. Sally was among them. Tess and I immediately hit it off and were engaged within six weeks."

"Blimey," said Mike. "You were a fast worker. Sally kept me waiting for eighteen months. I asked her to marry me, but she was a primary school teacher, and I was digging holes in the ground for a living. I think she was waiting for a better offer."

"I heard that," Sally called from the kitchen.

"You're still together," said Gus. "Tess and I were married in Salisbury Registry Office on Bourne Hill in 1980 and had thirty-five happy years together. Somehow, we didn't become another statistic to add to the long list of failed marriages where one partner was a police officer."

"Thirty-five years," said Mike. "You lost your wife in 2015. That must have been tough."

"We'd retired to a village near Devizes and were getting used to not having to dash off to work every day when Tess dropped dead right out of the blue. We had no warning whatsoever. You're right, it was tough for the next three years, but then I got an offer I couldn't refuse. I returned to work with the police as a consultant reviewing cold cases. John Crees and Mandy Howard are the latest ones to land on my desk. I'm hoping you can tell me much more about

John than I've found in the murder file from the original investigation."

"Did you live and work in Salisbury for the whole of that thirty-five years?" asked Mike. "I hadn't heard Sally mention your name. Of course, we've only lived here since 2006. I was born in Shaftesbury, and Sally taught in Blandford Forum when we met. I didn't have my own business back then. I was labouring for a firm that got the contract for a new sports hall and drama studio at her big comprehensive. We moved around a fair bit within Dorset after we married. I went where the work was, and Sally's profession gave her a good deal of flexibility. Even when Micky came along, she could keep teaching in some capacity."

"Tess and I lived in Laverstock at first and moved to Downton to live for several years," said Gus. "But my heart was always in Salisbury. I knew every narrow street and alleyway in the city, who to ask for information, and who to avoid. I enjoyed the cut and thrust with the local villains, and when I retired, I felt I'd solved a decent percentage of cases."

"I get the feeling you knew of John Crees, even if you hadn't met him in person," said Mike.

"Everyone at Bourne Hill knew Spider Crees by reputation," said Gus. "The tattoos made sure nobody who lived in the city was unaware of who was roaring past them on his Harley Davidson. I wasn't involved in the murder case, so I don't know a thing about Crees before he arrived in the city, nor why his life was taken in such a savage manner. That's where I'm hoping you can help."

Mike leaned back further into the cushions behind him and closed his eyes.

"What I saw when I turned on that bedroom light is as

clear today as it was six years ago," said Mike Woodman. "It was carnage."

"I can imagine," said Gus. "Tell me how John came to be working for you, Mike."

"It's a long story," said Mike. "My parents split up when I was thirteen. Two years later, my mother remarried. Her new husband had a son, a couple of years younger than me, Tim. He lived with his mother, but we got on well whenever he visited his father. After we'd left school and gone our different ways, we lost touch. Then, about fifteen years ago, Tim contacted me, and after we'd talked about what we'd been doing with our lives, Tim said he was looking to invest in a business. His mother had also married again. His stepfather was loaded. The family had lived in Surbiton, Surrey, and when his mother died, Tim inherited a tidy sum from the house sale. Tim wasn't interested in joining me in the labouring game, but he's been a silent partner ever since. His injection of capital allowed me to branch out on my own. I started employing people in 2003, was able to bid for bigger contracts, and things worked out well for both of us. But, as I said, Sally and I didn't move to Wessex Road until 2006. John told me he had arrived in Salisbury five years earlier. John originally came from Portsmouth and left school with good qualifications, but his home life wasn't happy, which is a familiar tale, no doubt, to a policeman like yourself. His mother and father split up when John was six, and although his mother found another bloke soon enough, he never took to his stepfather. John told me the guy was arrogant and controlling. The older John got, the more his stepfather resented having him in the house. So, John ran away at sixteen and found a job at a garage, where his love for motorcycles began. He bought a bike as soon as he got the money together."

"Where did he live, do you know?" asked Gus.

"Basingstoke," said Mike. "That was where he ran to when he left home. John was sleeping in a storeroom above the garage. Then, he met a local girl, Millie Trask, and got her pregnant. Their daughter, Polly, was born four months after John and Millie married in the summer of 1990. The family approached a housing association and secured a first-floor flat. John said the first eighteen months were the happiest he'd been since his father walked out. Then, someone moved out, and the flat below them on the ground floor was then occupied by a man living alone in his fifties. Neighbours told John the new tenant was a heroin user and dealer. Things started getting worse six months later. Someone smashed the guy's window, and John came home from the garage one day to find it boarded up.

"Did they report it to the police or complain to the housing association?" asked Gus.

"The housing association didn't seem interested," said Mike. "John tried ringing them from work but never spoke to a human being. He kept hearing a recorded message telling him his call was important to them, but they never picked up. John was already wary of the police."

"Was he involved with a motorcycle club in Basingstoke?" asked Gus.

"John didn't go into details, but he had started smoking cannabis soon after leaving home. So, he had his reasons for steering clear of the law. The dealer's flat attracted a lot of undesirables, as you can imagine. Anyone looking to score would use the window to enter the property downstairs, which made loads of noise. Eventually, the tenant was evicted from the flat, but John told me the flat door had been off its hinges so often due to police raids that it was insecure. Everything changed overnight. John said he was soon living in constant fear for his family. He was terrified of waking to find Polly gone after squatters moved into the now vacant flat. People came and went all night, shouting, screaming, and banging on walls. Polly's bedroom was directly above the front door, and she came into John and Millie's room because she was scared to sleep in her bed."

"I would never have realised from the murder file," said Gus. "I'm seeing a different side of John Crees. That must have been hell for him."

"The John Crees people saw after he'd arrived in Salisbury soon had the spider tattoos and the customised Harley," said Mike. "John and Mandy were bikers, but he was far less menacing than he looked. I could never understand why the police believed they'd fallen out with the Hells Angels. It didn't make sense."

"Fair enough," said Gus. "Did things improve for the family, or is there more to hear?"

"A month after the shouting and screaming incident, they were subjected to a terrifying ordeal when the squatters tried to break into his home," said Mike. "John heard them outside the door, shouting they would kill him. The men squatting in the flat locked themselves inside during the day and only removed the padlock and chain at night. John and Millie lived in constant fear of what would happen next. They had been together for almost two years, and the situation always caused arguments. John told me he felt he was doing an inadequate job protecting his wife and daughter. The housing association tried to evict the squatters, but John was told it could take another two months. He didn't know if they could stand another two months. So he withheld his rent because he reckoned it had been going on for too long, and they weren't doing enough. You can guess what happened. The housing association threatened to evict him, and it proved the last straw. Millie took their daughter with her back to her parents."

"Did John continue to work at the garage and live in Basingstoke?" asked Gus.

"For a month or two," said Mike Woodburn. "Then he quit and joined the Army."

"That would have been in 1993, am I right?" asked Gus.

"Correct," said Mike. "Six years later, the Army was in Kosovo. Ethnic Albanians comprise ninety percent of the Kosovo population, and the Serbs had historically viewed the region as part of their country. In February 1999, four thousand British troops had been committed to a NATO peace-keeping force. John Crees was among them as they gathered in neighbouring Macedonia."

"I remember the bombing started soon after," said Gus. "NATO targeted military positions in Serbia and Kosovo after deploying special forces personnel to locate targets. The bombing went ahead without UN Security Council approval, leading to hundreds of civilian deaths."

"John witnessed the results of the bombing, and it affected him deeply," said Mike.

"Milosevic stepped up the aggression, and soon there was a refugee crisis as a million Albanians poured across the borders into Macedonia and Albania."

"John's company was sent to help the aid agencies. They erected tents, distributed food, and provided medical assistance."

"How long before John came home?" asked Gus.

"He flew home in October and left the Army in the New Year," said Mike. "John told me he bought his first Harley Davidson, drove through Basingstoke without stopping, and arrived in Salisbury. After his experiences over the past six years, he switched to a far more laid-back lifestyle, a world away from the regimented routine of Army life. John said he'd had a couple of tattoos done on his body as a teenager, but no spiders until he'd spent time in Kosovo."

"Tattoos have never appealed to me," said Gus. "What did he see in Kosovo that convinced him to cover himself in spider tattoos?"

"Perhaps it was the cannabis," said Mike. "John admitted he was smoking more after coming home. Cross Orbweavers are the most common there, or so he told me. All the tattoos on his body and that bike of his were the same species."

"Cannabis is another thing that never appealed," said Gus. "So, John found work as a labourer, in and around Salisbury, for five years before you moved here."

"That's right," said Mike. "John was capable of so much more. His grades in his exams put mine to shame, but he was happiest outside, in all winds and weather, working for someone else. He wasn't ambitious, didn't want responsibilities, and just wanted to live on his terms."

"How soon after you moved to this house did John come to work for you?" asked Gus.

"I had several labourers on my books then, but a couple of blokes were getting on a bit. They didn't want to travel thirty miles a day back and forth from the next county, so I advertised in the Journal. John phoned the same night the ad appeared, along with another chap, and they started with me the following Monday. We hadn't finished opening boxes here, so it must have been less than a month after the move. John never let me down. He was always on time, worked hard throughout the day, and was polite to anyone he met on our various sites."

"I imagine he'd been working for someone else before

you took him on," said Gus. "Any reason for him jumping ship, especially to a new face in the city?"

"Labourers often have to move from one small firm to another. Then, once the initial groundwork's done, other skills move on site to carry out the next stages."

"Either he had to be happy to work a couple of days a week, or he found a bigger firm with a succession of rolling contracts meaning labourers moved from site to site without a break."

"Exactly, and the only reason I could afford to move here was because I had built a good reputation," said Mike. "John stayed with me from then on because I offered him security. I trusted John and encouraged him to add to his skillset. He was cool with it as long as he was still one of the lads. In case you were wondering, there was no animosity between John and the firm he left at short notice in 2006."

"After a couple of years with you, John met Mandy Howard," said Gus. "Did he ever mention meeting her while he was at work?"

"Not a word," said Mike. "I saw the pair of them riding on Wain-along-Road one Sunday afternoon on their bikes while walking with Sally. It was unusual to see just the two bikes. John rode with the local club. A dozen bikes would regularly drive through parts of the city in convoy at week-ends, and you couldn't mistake John among them when they roared past."

"John had spoken to you about Millie and Polly," said Gus. "When he and Mandy started to spend more time together, did you ever wonder what had happened to their marriage?"

"Of course," said Mike, "but John's private life was his own business. I didn't pry. But, when he was ready to take things further with Mandy, he told me Millie had asked for a divorce six months after he joined the Army. John had no clue where Millie and their daughter had gone in the years since, and I gathered he'd reconciled his feelings about things and had moved on. The divorce was finalised in 1994. He was free to marry Mandy, but they were content to live together for the time being. John and Mandy moved into Rampart Road in 2010 and continued to ride their bikes every weekend."

"What about the local clubhouse? Did they spend a lot of time there?" asked Gus.

"What? The two properties knocked into one?" asked Mike. "I don't think John ever went there. He knew of it, but that crowd was hard-core, not his style."

"Did you ever meet Mandy?" asked Gus.

"Only in passing," said Mike. "Once John told me they were in a relationship, they would wave out as they drove past whenever I saw them on their bikes. I spoke to John daily at work, but we didn't socialise."

"Did John ever tell you why Mandy came to Salisbury from South Wales?" asked Gus. "Her family lived in Merthyr, and there was nothing in the murder file to suggest she had ever married. An admin assistant's role can cover all manner of clerical tasks, but it's not a senior position. Her move wasn't due to a promotion. Mandy swapped her role with the council in Merthyr for the same job in a city over a hundred miles away. A place where she had no friends or relatives."

"Have you been to Merthyr, Gus?" asked Mike.

"A recent case took us to the area, Mike. The surrounding countryside is beautiful, but although the mining industry is long gone, it has left scars on the landscape."

"A very diplomatic answer," said Mike. "Mandy

wouldn't have been the first to take the M4 out of Wales looking for streets paved with gold instead of coal dust. She had probably heard a legion of sad stories about girls her age who dreamt London was the place to go. Salisbury is a beautiful city and a far more peaceful environment than the English capital. It was here that she found her soulmate in John Crees. Someone who wanted the same unconventional lifestyle and was happy in their own skin, not bothering anyone, and just asking the same in return."

"The original investigation searched high and low for someone who thought theirs was a life-choice they should die for," said Gus. "They had no luck whatsoever."

"I wish I could help you further, Gus," said Mike. "John and I said goodbye on what proved to be his last Friday night. I didn't happen to see John and Mandy that weekend, despite many bikers on the city streets, and then on Monday morning, he wasn't waiting for his lift. You know the rest."

"I may be back later, Mike," said Gus. "I'm meeting one of the detectives in the case at eleven, so I'd best get back to Bourne Hill. Maybe I'll drive to a building site for a chat next time. I hope you're back on your feet again soon. I'll pop next door to say cheerio to Sally and thank her for the refreshments."

Two minutes later, Sally Woodman saw Gus to the front door.

"Good to see you again after all these years, Gus," she said. "I hope you find the person responsible."

"So do I, Sally," said Gus. "Time is ticking, and my consultancy role has an invisible expiry date. I know it's there, but I can't make it out yet. I want to solve every cold case, to close the book on it finally, but because this double murder happened here, on my doorstep, I want to solve this one more than any I've ever tackled."

"You'll get there, Gus," said Sally. "Tess always said you would never admit you were beaten. There was always another thread to follow, which might result in a positive outcome, no matter how slender the chances looked."

"That's me," said Gus. "As long as I never ran out of threads, I was fine."

Gus walked along Wessex Road on his way back to Bourne Hill. Sally closed the door, entered the lounge to make Mike comfortable, and asked what he fancied for lunch.

"IT'S WARMER INSIDE than out, Gus," said Bob Martin as Gus entered Reception. "Any joy?"

"Too soon to tell, Bob," said Gus. "I've got a better idea of one of the victims, but it differs markedly from the murder file. I'm not sure what that's about. Phil Crocker wasn't upstairs when I arrived this morning. Have you seen him?"

"It's Friday," said Bob. "Let me check the book. He's in court this morning and off this afternoon."

"Typical," said Gus. "I need a lockable filing cabinet."

"There's bound to be an empty one in someone's cubicle up there," said Bob. "Bob Mears is in. Have a word with him. He'll sort you out."

"I'm meeting Mears in three minutes," said Gus. "I'd better get a wiggle on. Do you know which care home Jeff Sheppard is in, by the way? I want to visit him."

"I'll find out, Gus," said Bob. "I finish at one today, but I'll leave the details with my opposite number."

Gus gave Bob a thumbs up and took the stairs to the first-floor. Bob Mears was already just outside Gus's cubicle.

He watched Bob stand beside the desk, then slide open the top drawer.

"Bang on time, Bob, that's good," said Gus, who narrowed the gap as quickly as possible. "What were you after, paperclips?"

"I've got enough of my own, thanks," said Mears. "It's rare to see a clear desk top, that's all."

"Bob Martin reckoned you could point me towards a lockable filing cabinet I could use," said Gus. "My colleague and I will need somewhere to store the new information we gather next week."

"That sounds like you don't trust the detectives working here," said Mears. "You wouldn't want that getting out."

"We're not here to win friends, Bob. The case might be six years old, but if we identify the culprit, whoever takes the case to court will need to maintain continuity and security. Since I returned to work, I tend to count the number of sheets in the murder file at the outset. That means I only have to count the fresh sheets we print off when we're done."

"I have other cases that demand my attention," said Mears. "Let's get on with whatever you want to ask me, and then I'll find a filing cabinet where you can lock your precious files."

"Thank you, Bob," said Gus. "Run me through events on the evening of Monday the twenty-second of October 2012. When did you get the call?"

Bob flopped into the guest chair liked a petulant schoolboy.

"Phil and I were working on burglaries from electrical shops," said Mears. "A couple of shops in the city centre had been hit, and then they targeted a major supplier on the Churchfields Industrial Estate. It happens most years in the run-up to Christmas."

"Thieves know the businesses will increase their stock levels in anticipation of a rush," said Gus. "They remove as much as possible and offer TVs and games at discounted prices on market stalls and car boots."

"Most of the culprits are too thick to make it difficult for us, but we still have to do the legwork," said Mears. "Phil received a tip-off, and we were heading for an address in Wilton when we got the call. When we arrived on Rampart Road, uniforms were securing the scene, an ambulance was pulling away, and the Police Surgeon's car was parked outside the house where the murder occurred."

"Who called the ambulance?" asked Gus.

"The bloke who dialled 999. Don't know why he bothered with an ambulance."

"Mike Woodman," said Gus. "John Crees's employer found the bodies upstairs in the front bedroom. What did you do first, speak to Mike, or follow Dr Sheppard upstairs?"

"Phil went upstairs, and I spoke to the uniforms. They told me what Woodman told them, and I then spoke with him. He confirmed the victim's identity and told me the sequence of events after he first suspected foul play. Phil came downstairs soon after, and I could tell how bad it was from the look on his face. It takes a lot to affect Phil, but you've seen the photos in your precious murder file. Whoever did that was an animal."

"What did Phil ask to be done next?" asked Gus.

"We started house-to-house enquiries along Rampart Road," said Mears. "There were no sounds of a struggle or screams coming from the house between Saturday night and Monday evening. We didn't know when the couple died at that point, so we covered all bases."

"That stretch of Rampart Road didn't help either," said Gus.

"The main road is a busy stretch, all day and most of the night," said Mears. "The traffic noise would mask any sounds of a struggle, even without considering how loud some of the older people on that road have their tellies."

"What did you do next?" asked Gus.

"We returned on Tuesday, and spread the net wider, asking if anyone had seen suspicious activity in the week leading up to midnight on Saturday the twentieth," said Mears. "Uniforms talked to people we missed on Monday night too, but nothing useful turned up. Phil spoke to the media after time-of-death became clearer. He appealed for witnesses who noticed anybody in the early hours of Sunday near Rampart Road with heavily bloodstained clothing. The killer could not have carried out such a ferocious attack and not been covered in blood. Nobody came forward."

"How soon was Jeff Sheppard prepared to describe the missing murder weapon?" asked Gus.

"On Friday morning, if I remember right. It will be in your file. Uniformed officers had already searched for anything described as a blunt-force instrument. Not just inside the house or the garden, and found nothing. So Phil called for a specialist team to search the drains, rubbish tips, and disturb koi carp in a back garden pond half a mile away."

"No matter where you looked, the four-pound lump hammer, or a similar object, never turned up," said Gus.

"Phil thinks you believe we missed something obvious," said Mears. "We tried to think of everything. His first idea was the couple had been murdered during the course of a robbery. That wasn't such a daft idea. Mike Woodman had told us John Crees had brought home a wage packet on Friday evening. We didn't find large amounts of cash at the property. Crees had nothing except keys in the pockets of his trousers by the side of the bed. Mandy Howard's purse contained a five-pound note and loose change. They kept themselves to themselves, so none of the neighbours knew whether the couple had jewellery or valuable watches in the house, but there was no evidence of anyone rifling through drawers or clothing searching for something worth stealing. As Phil pointed out, a simple robbery wouldn't explain the horrific level of violence used. The attack had to be personal. All the injuries were inflicted on the head and face."

"So, with a level of violence that seemed overkill, you and Phil switched your attention to the lifestyle Crees and Howard led and the people they mixed with. When I read a summary of the investigation, I sensed you quickly became fixated on the biker community."

"It was a legitimate line of enquiry," said Mears. "John Crees rode with the local club for five years before Mandy moved to Salisbury. Several of the members of that club were known to be involved in criminal activity. You worked at Bourne Hill for most of your career, so you know a few unsavoury characters rode with that crowd."

"Perhaps I was fortunate," said Gus, "but I was never directly involved in a case where one of the brethren was a prime suspect. What I do remember, though, are other detectives closer to the action who told me that because the motorcycle clubs were such a closed shop, it was difficult to stifle their activities."

"A closed shop is putting it mildly," said Mears. "If an

investment opportunity arose for a major drug shipment, our local bike club could apply for central funds. Do you remember where they generated the war chest they accumulated?"

"I never went anywhere near Long Marston," said Gus. "A Detective Inspector at London Road reckoned the now defunct annual Bulldog Bash provided millions in profits."

"If central funds were sanctioned for use in Salisbury, it was impossible to trace where it had originated, even if we caught them red-handed," said Mears. "We started interviewing club members after raiding their clubhouse on Milford Hill."

"What did you find?" asked Gus.

"Trouble," said Mears.

## Chapter Seven

"YOU DISTURBED A HORNET'S NEST," said Gus. "Which led to you and Phil receiving thinly disguised intimidation."

"We interviewed two dozen bikers," said Mears. "They were uncooperative, as you can imagine. The raid turned up an assortment of drugs and offensive weapons. We found cash that couldn't readily be explained and enough motorcycle spares and accessories to open a shop. The club bar had booze and cigarettes from overseas that had somehow escaped paying duty as it crossed our border."

"Phil Crocker told me at the time that they had knocked down the party wall and installed a snooker table on the first floor," said Gus. "Was there any truth in that?"

"Yes, they had. Cheeky beggars," said Mears. "The cloth on the table was as good you get at the Crucible for the World Championships, and the light box was top-of-the-range too. The guys playing when we burst in didn't have to duck to avoid bashing their head on the heavy shade like in the snooker club in the city."

"I'm guessing the raid didn't result in a shedload of charges," said Gus.

"Bits and pieces," said Mears. "As for connecting anyone with the murder, that was impossible. We got a string of no comments, and despite interviewing hundreds of other people who lived close to the clubhouse, we never uncovered a potential suspect. The longer those interviews continued, the more I doubted the club members had a motive."

"John Crees was one of the ninety-nine percent," said Gus. "He wasn't a criminal, had never attended the clubhouse, and stopped riding with the club members at weekends after Mandy Howard arrived in Salisbury."

"On the Monday following the interviews relating to the raid, Phil thought we should try another angle," said Mears. "But the intimidation had started over the weekend. Every biker associated with that club rode past my house, one after another, the second I turned the bedside light out on Friday night."

"What was Phil's idea for a new angle?" asked Gus.

"He thought we should pursue the suggestion the murder was drug-related," said Mears. "Not necessarily connected to the motorcycle club, but Crees and Howard were known users. Phil wanted to learn whether Crees had graduated to dealing and foolishly operated on another guy's turf."

"That sounds like a possible working theory," said Gus. "But as with other theories thrown into the mix back in 2012, it didn't explain the level of violence used."

"The press jumped on the drug connection," said Mears. "That became the focus of every article they published, which left friends and neighbours of the couple angry. They said the coverage didn't reflect the true character of the freewheeling duo they knew. They complained it would lead to a lack of public sympathy for the victims. Ultimately, it might even discourage potential witnesses from coming forward."

"Did you and Phil ever pursue that fresh angle?" asked Gus.

"We were distracted by the number of bikers and the frequency with which they passed our homes. The theory the murders were drug-related remained exactly that, just a theory. Several suspected drug dealers, and some we had arrested and imprisoned, were interviewed and eliminated from our enquiries. We remained optimistic there was someone out there with the information that could help solve the murders, but we never found them in the time we were allowed. The days ticked by, and our superiors kept an eye on the costs of keeping us safe. My wife was scared a biker would lob a Molotov cocktail through our front room window at any minute, even if patrol cars were cruising our streets."

"Did the intimidation ever go beyond just riding past your houses?" asked Gus.

"No," said Mears shaking his head. "That was why it was so damaging to the investigation. If we'd had a fire-bombing or received death threats in the post, our superiors would have had to take action. Instead, those bikers took every precaution possible to keep within the law. They stayed under the speed limit; and didn't sound any air horns they might have had in the early hours. There was no verbal abuse. Nothing but a string of bikes slowly riding past our front door. Fellow detectives walked past us here at Bourne Hill with their heads down, always looking busy. Nobody wanted to get landed with taking over the investigation if the bosses decided to take us out of the firing line."

"I was investigating a series of sex attacks at the local

college," said Gus. "I remember there being an atmosphere, a feeling of unease in the building, but I can't recall there being a rumour you two would be replaced."

"I came into the office one Monday morning, just after Christmas," said Mears. "Phil told me he'd just seen an Assistant Chief Constable leaving our superior's office. The ACC had been inside for fifteen minutes, tops. It was plain something was happening. We thought we were being replaced, but when we were called into his office, our boss told us to ensure everything was written up, wrap up the investigation, and handed us another case."

"Did the intimidation stop?" asked Gus.

"Within twenty-four hours," said Mears. "The ACC gave a press conference later on Monday morning. He stressed that although several lines of enquiry had been followed assiduously, and hundreds of witness statements had been taken, it hadn't been possible at this stage to identify any suspects or find the murder weapon. So he appealed for anyone with information they had so far withheld, for whatever reason, to come forward. The file would stay open, and we wouldn't rest until the killer of John Crees and Mandy Howard was found. He didn't admit that we hadn't even identified a true motive, but the one positive Phil and I could take was the bikes didn't come back after Monday night."

"Where would Phil have steered the investigation that week if you hadn't had the rug pulled out from under you by the ACC?"

"Phil wanted to dig deeper into John Crees's Basingstoke connections," said Mears. "That was when the cannabis use started in earnest. Also, he wanted to speak to our colleagues in Merthyr Tydfil again. We'd already asked whether Mandy Howard or her family had ever crossed their path. She had never been in trouble with the law, and all her relatives were squeaky clean."

"I asked Mike Woodman, Crees's ex-boss, why Mandy Howard moved to Salisbury," said Gus. "He didn't have the information you and Phil had, but as he pointed out, all manner of young men and women move away from their home town to find work, especially if the economy in the area where they live is declining. Merthyr Tydfil was once the economic capital of Wales, the heart of a thriving iron and coal industry. When Mandy Howard left school, the town had become a byword for deprivation as the traditional industries had crashed and burned. Few new ones emerged to take their place in the decade before she left home. Less than two-thirds of working-aged people were in employment. More than forty per cent of those described as economically inactive were classified as long-term sick, a figure twice the national average."

"You seem to know a lot about the place," said Mears.

"My team and I spent time in the area on a case earlier in the year. I made a point of watching an item on a regional TV programme. It was a useful background for the people we were investigating. The way people live can influence the way they act. Since Mandy left home, over a thousand jobs have been created in the borough. Maybe things would have been different for her if she'd stuck it out. Light industrial factories have opened in the past six years, and a large retail park features big high-street names. There are plenty of places for an admin assistant to find work or seek a career change. Millions have been spent on regeneration programmes across the borough, including in the Merthyr town centre. Merthyr is developing into a modern commercial hub with a lot to offer locals and visitors."

"How does that help you with your cold case review," said Mears. "Mandy Howard died here in Salisbury."

"We won't know the answer to that until we ask the right questions of the right people, Bob," said Gus.

"Was there anything else?" asked Mears.

"That filing cabinet," said Gus. "I'm off to find someone who worked with Mandy Howard in one of the council offices. Can you point me in the right direction?"

"Housing," said Mears. "That was the department she worked in. Your filing cabinet, and the keys, will be here when you get back."

Bob Mears made his way back across the office, and Gus donned his overcoat, ready to venture outside. He wondered whether Bob had believed him when he said he'd counted the number of individual sheets in the file folder. Gus left the cubicle after moving the folder from the top drawer to the bottom, just in case.

A quick check of the signs outside led him to the Housing Department offices. It took almost as long to gain access as it did on a bad day at London Road, but after three separate managers had checked his ID, Gus was permitted to speak to Emily Farrell, a housing officer.

"Good afternoon, Emily. My name's Gus Freeman," said Gus. "I'm a consultant working for Wiltshire Police. I understand you worked here in October 2012 when Amanda Howard was murdered."

"That's right," said Emily. "I've worked in the Housing Department since 2008. Mandy joined us the following year. She had moved from South Wales to come to live in Salisbury. We were glad to have her join us, this department is always busy, and she didn't require training. Mandy had fulfilled the same role in the council offices in the Civic Centre on Castle Street in Merthyr Tydfil."

"So I understand, Emily," said Gus. "Did you think it odd Mandy moved so far for so little change?"

"I'm not sure I know what you mean, Mr Freeman," said Emily.

"Well, there wouldn't be much salary difference between South Wales and Salisbury. Mandy wasn't moving due to a promotion, was she? Also, Mandy lived with her parents in Merthyr, and even if she paid the going rate for her contribution to the family housekeeping, it would be nothing like the cost of renting a flat here in the city. As a housing officer, you would be aware of the problems she faced."

"I hadn't thought of it that way," said Emily. "Mandy was a good worker. She only had perhaps one or two days off sick throughout the year. I suppose I assumed she moved for a change of scenery. You know what they say about the word assume."

"I do," said Gus. "Did Mandy socialise with you and others from these council offices?"

"There's not so much of that these days," said Emily. "When I started for the council in 2004, the lady in this role talked about enjoying get-togethers for the office staff. That would have been in the 80s. People live different lives these days and travel further to get to work. Quite a few of my colleagues drive from towns and villages outside the city. Thirty minutes to get to and from work is one thing; to repeat the trip for a few soft drinks and a game of skittles in the evening is another thing altogether."

"The drink-drive law put paid to many social occasions, I imagine," said Gus.

"It wasn't just that," said Emily. "My old boss said that at Christmas after everyone had been to the pub at lunchtime, it was like Sodom and Gomorrah in these offices. She needed to knock half a dozen times before opening a door, you know? The bosses don't encourage staff to do anything that might bring the council into disrepute."

"I get the picture," said Gus, glancing towards the photocopier in the corner. "Did Mandy meet anyone after she first worked here?"

"I got the feeling there was no one special until Mandy met John. They were kindred spirits. They both loved their bikes and being on the open road. We rarely saw one another outside of work, but it didn't surprise me when Mandy came in one Monday morning to say she needed to notify me of a change of address."

"What did you make of John Crees and those spider tattoos?" asked Gus.

"I don't often get to say this in my job, Mr Freeman. Live and let live, that's what I thought. When Mandy talked about John, it was clear he was a gentle man, kind, generous, and hard-working. In other words, the complete opposite of the image he showed to the world. People saw what they wanted to see."

"Did Mandy always own a bike?" asked Gus.

"How do you think she got to Salisbury in the first place, Mr Freeman? Mandy told me she spotted the vacancy, applied for it, and handed in her notice as soon as she learned she had been successful. Her father sent her belongings by train direct from Cardiff to Salisbury. When she and John moved in together, they ferried her things across the city on their bikes."

"That sounds like her relationship with her family was good," said Gus. "Did she go back often to visit?"

"Mandy phoned her mother most weekends," said Emily. "I don't think there was a problem with her father, but she never mentioned going home, not to me. Of course, we didn't always have time for a chat; it was so busy."

"What is your role, Emily, and how did Mandy fit into it?" asked Gus.

"We assess the needs of people applying for housing," said Emily, "and give them vacant accommodation when available. In addition, we conduct regular inspections and deal with anti-social behaviour and broken tenancy agreements."

"That could cause arguments, I imagine," said Gus. "You might think the tenant was at fault, and they might take a different view. Can you remember anyone who argued with Mandy?"

"I would have made the decision, Mr Freeman," said Emily. "if they had a go at anyone, it would have been me. I can't believe anything that happened here would have caused someone to murder Mandy as they did. John died too, and although he was a gentle man, many of the tenants we deal with wouldn't be capable of tackling a man the size of John."

"A fair point," said Gus. "Although, they were likely to have been asleep when the attack occurred. What other activities do you carry out that bring you face-to-face with members of the public?"

"Nothing dangerous," said Emily. "We refer people for advice on benefits and welfare, set rents, and deal with payments and arrears. Mandy's role was to provide administrative and organisational support to me as Housing Officer. That involved many operational and support services focusing on our tenants. Everything is geared to help us deliver high-quality, responsive and consistent services. Mandy was good at that. I miss her."

"I'm sure the detectives asked you this question, Emily," said Gus. "Can you remember anything different happening in the week leading to the murder?"

"They asked all of us whether we saw any unfamiliar faces in the offices, outside in the car park, that sort of thing. Was there anyone following Mandy when she walked to work or when she walked home."

"Mandy walked to work. That makes sense," said Gus. "I lived in Salisbury as a boy, and Mandy could walk from Rampart Road to this office in ten minutes. It would take almost as long to ride here. Why waste money on petrol? So, nothing seemed strange that week?"

"None of us could remember seeing anyone we didn't recognise in the building," said Emily. "We're like a doctor's surgery, and we see a lot of frequent flyers. Nobody remembered seeing anyone following Mandy either."

"Did you ever visit the Winchester Gate pub where Mandy worked?" asked Gus.

"I don't drink," said Emily. "I live the other side of Netherhampton and travel the four miles on the bus daily during the week."

Gus decided not to ask whether Emily visited Salisbury Racecourse, which was on her doorstep, if she lived near Netherhampton. Gambling was probably another thing Emily didn't do. How many more dead ends would there be in this case?

"I think that's all the questions I have for now, Emily," said Gus. "Thanks for sparing the time. If you suddenly remember something you think might be important, pop next door, and leave a message with a sergeant at Reception. A colleague and I are moving in next Monday to continue the investigation."

"I can't imagine I'll remember anything new after so long," said Emily. "I'll never forget that Tuesday afternoon. We hadn't heard from her on Monday, and it was rare for Mandy to take a day off sick, as I told you, but we were extra busy, being one short, and I phoned her mid-morning but got no reply. I was returning from lunch, and as I came through the front door, someone told me they'd heard Mandy and her partner were dead. My first thought was they'd had an accident on their motorbikes. When I saw the news on the television in the evening, it was shocking to hear what happened to them. How could anyone do that? Ever since that night, I've tried to forget what I heard. I can't start going over it in my head again, Mr Freeman, remembering how she was when she was sat at that desk behind you."

"Don't torture yourself, Emily," said Gus. "You might not have a snippet of valuable information hidden away in that head of yours. But, if you do, it could help us identify her killer. We are unsure whether John and Mandy were targeted for a reason we never discovered. Perhaps it was a random attack. If so, the killer could strike again, and your snippet of information might save another person's life."

Emily shivered.

"I know you mean well, Mr Freeman," she said. "Reminding me the killer is still out there doesn't help."

Gus realised he was fighting a losing battle. He said his goodbyes to the nervous Housing Officer, buttoned his overcoat, and returned to the police station. He spotted a two-drawer grey filing cabinet beside the desk as he approached his cubicle. A ring with two keys lay on the top. Gus checked the desk's bottom drawer, but the folder didn't appear touched.

He transferred it to the filing cabinet, locked it, and attached the keys to his bunch from the Old Police Station office. Gus made a mental note to give the spare key to Blessing on Monday morning. A movement to his left made him look across the room. DCI Phil Crocker was in his office. Perhaps it was time to build bridges.

"Good afternoon, sir," said Gus. "Bob Mears and I had a fruitful discussion this morning. He found me a lockable cabinet too, which will be most useful. So far, I've interviewed Mike Woodman, John Crees's employer, and Emily Farrell, who worked with Mandy Howard in the Housing Department. I was just about to locate Jeff Sheppard, the police surgeon, to arrange to meet him on Monday."

"You'll find him at Holmwood House," said Phil Crocker. "Jeff moved into a retirement home. Assisted living, they call it, where he can cope most of the time alone, but someone's there if he needs them. Probably cost him a fortune. Did you learn anything new from Woodman and the Housing woman?"

"I've learned John Crees wasn't the demon biker portrayed by the press," said Gus. "Twice today, I've heard him described as a gentle man. Did you ever wonder whether the raid on the Milford Hill clubhouse sparked the ride-by intimidation you and Bob attracted? I'm not convinced it had anything to do with John being involved with the biker community. From what I've heard, John was comfortable riding with the motorcycle club members at weekends before Mandy Howard arrived on the scene, but he never set foot in that clubhouse and steered clear of any of the criminal activities going on under its roof. As soon as he got together with Mandy, he completely severed his connection with the club."

"Maybe it was the drugs all along," said Crocker. "We were told to drop the case before I could get back to Basingstoke to see whether Crees was dealing as well as using. He had to have upset someone big time at some point in his life. I thought about his time in the Army too. What if he killed someone out there in Kosovo? Many people died at the hands of the Serbs, but it wouldn't be the first time a British soldier was accused of killing a civilian in a foreign country. The trouble is the Army closes ranks and makes it impossible to speak to anyone."

"Did you think it likely, sir?" asked Gus.

"Not really. I was clutching at straws," sighed DCI Crocker.

"I'll give the care home a call," said Gus. "Once I've set up a meeting with Jeff Sheppard, I think I'll call it a day."

Phil Crocker looked at his watch.

"Nice work if you can get it. I'll be lucky to get away before six."

"I've only scratched the surface on that weighty file folder, sir," said Gus. "The roads will be quieter, and I can dig deeper into the detail in those reports at home. These cubicles might be on-trend, but they affect your concentration level. People wander by, engaged in idle banter or chatting on their phones. I hope two hours of quiet reading in my lounge before my better half returns will pay dividends next week."

"Your better half?" asked Phil Crocker. "I didn't realise you'd married again."

"I haven't," said Gus. "For almost three years after Tess died, I was a mess. Everything we'd planned for our retirement had been torn away in an instant. I floundered around like a goldfish that had leapt out of its bowl."

"We were surprised you moved away from Salisbury," said Crocker. "You both had a network of friends and acquaintances in the city to help you through the grieving process."

"Tess agreed we needed a clean break from this place," said Gus. "We'd found the ideal spot in Urchfont, and having already enjoyed a slice of village life in Downton, we knew what it took to fit in. Fate decided we would only have six months to gain the trust of the good people of Urchfont. Thanks to a handful of those villagers, I coped with her loss. When Kenneth Truelove contacted me, I was quite prepared to ignore him. I didn't have a clue what he had in mind. I imagined it was a routine welfare call, but I thought I had nothing to lose by dropping into London Road for a coffee and a chat."

"You thought they were worried you might be a suicide candidate," said Phil Crocker. "The statistics back that up. Some coppers can't let it be after they pack in. They spend all their time with ex-coppers, playing golf, drinking, and cruising. I won't be dragged down that rabbit-hole when I retire. That way lies madness and a short step to wondering whether you could stomach the boredom for another decade. So, when you learned what Kenneth had in mind, what made you decide to take him up on his offer?"

"Geoff Mercer played a big part in my decision," said Gus. "Although I'd never tell him so. We didn't always get on, but he'd changed for the better, and the youngsters Geoff and Kenneth had earmarked for the Crime Review Team struck me as being above par. We've both been lumbered with junior officers who were green as grass and would never reach the standard we required, but I sensed real promise with my original three."

"How you've managed to increase the size of that team against a background of cuts, cuts, and more cuts is nothing short of miraculous," said Crocker.

"We've continued to solve cases, sir," said Gus. "I imagine that's why you weren't best pleased to hear we were re-opening a case you and Bob Mears handled."

"We did our best," said Crocker. "It was the higher-ups

who pulled the plug. Whether my untested leads would have led us to the killer, I don't know. My biggest fear is that you'll do what we couldn't, uncover a motive, and find the killer. It will make us look bad, and when they finally decide where we're moving after they close Bourne Hill, our services will no longer be required."

"From what I've seen and read so far, it doesn't appear you missed something obvious, sir," said Gus. "If we find the key to unlocking this case, I don't mind betting it will be from a lead you didn't follow, and nobody can blame you for that. But, of course, there's always a first time that we might come up blank too."

"Well, we live in hope. Tell me to mind my own business, but you didn't elaborate on your better half. Heaven knows how I'd cop if I had to tackle the mysteries of the modern dating game. Did you join a lonely hearts club?"

Gus laughed.

"I was lonely, but I wasn't looking for anyone. Kenneth's PA took pity on me, and we spent time together for a few weeks once I'd agreed to return to work. We kept talking on the phone and bumping into one another at London Road. We both knew it wasn't a permanent arrangement. Then, out of the blue, a Detective Inspector reporting to Geoff Mercer came into my life. Suzie Ferris, have you ever worked with her, sir?"

"The name sounds familiar," said DCI Crocker. "I can't remember having met her, though. I thought I knew most people working at London Road. Those with as many years' service as Bob and me."

"Suzie's in her early thirties," said Gus. "We're expecting our first child in April."

"Blimey," said Phil Crocker.

"It was the last thing I ever thought would happen,"

said Gus. "Odd how things turn out. What she sees in me, I don't know, but I love her, we're happy, and long may it continue."

"Well, I hope everything continues to go well for you both," said Phil Crocker. "Look, I was rude to you when you first arrived. Bob and I will keep out of your hair for as long as you're working here. You'll get no interference from either of us, and we'll make sure the other detectives on this floor get the same message. You're one of the good guys, Gus. Even if I'm not overly keen on seeing you continue your run of success at my expense."

"Thank you, sir, I think," said Gus.

He returned to his desk and called Holmwood House.

Fifteen minutes later, he was ready to leave for Urchfont. Dr Sheppard had agreed to meet with Gus and DC Umeh at nine-fifteen on Monday morning.

# Chapter Eight

GUS DONNED HIS OVERCOAT, tucked the file folder under his arm, and trotted downstairs to the car park. His hopes for a quieter drive home in the middle of the afternoon were dented by a minor traffic accident in Shrewton. A milk float must have skidded on the icy road and overturned. There was broken glass everywhere on the right-hand-side of the narrow road through the village. It would be single-file traffic for several hours yet. Gus turned the Focus through the gateway of the bungalow a few minutes before three.

After a cup of coffee, he sat in the lounge with the murder file and prepared a set of questions for Jeff Sheppard. Gus remembered he and Suzie would be visiting Worton Farm in the morning. If Blessing was out of bed, he could run through the list with her. Five minutes tomorrow would save precious time on Monday morning. Holmwood House wasn't far from Bourne Hill nick, but Jeff's insistence they didn't disrupt his daily Tai Chi session at ten-thirty meant they were tight for time.

After suffering the traumas of the crime scene photos and Jeff Sheppard's autopsy report, Gus sought more information on Mandy Howard. Something had been troubling him ever since he had spoken with Emily Farrell.

Gus found a report of an interview his new pal, Phil Crocker, had with another council employee. Gillian Lye had been a year younger than Mandy Howard and worked in Adult Care. There was an address and a contact number in the file. He wondered whether it was too late to call today and then dialled the number anyway.

"Gillian Lye?" asked Gus.

"Yes. How may I help you?"

"My name is Gus Freeman, a consultant with Wiltshire Police. We've reopened the investigation into Mandy Howard's murder. I shall be working at Bourne Hill Police Station from Monday morning. I want to set up a meeting as soon as possible. When would be convenient?"

"I can be available Tuesday morning at ten o'clock," said Gillian. "My diary for the next three days would make it impossible to meet you before then, I'm afraid."

"I imagine you have to make home visits in your job," said Gus. "I understand, but as you and Mandy lived together for over a year, we must hear what you can tell us about her."

"I won't be popular with my boss," said Gillian, "but I'll book a half-day holiday on Tuesday. Do you have my home address?"

Gus checked the details from the murder file report were unchanged, and he told Gillian he would arrive in Hilltop Way at ten on Tuesday morning with a female colleague.

"Okay, see you then," said Gillian.

Gus ran through the report again and compiled another list of questions.

Phil Crocker had first asked Gillian Lye about her role with Adult Care for Salisbury Council.

"We support independent lives in our communities," she replied. "We always try to support people in their own homes, but sometimes people must move to more suitable accommodation to continue to live independently. We try to ensure there is always a range of accommodations that allows people to be supported at home. Social care services can appear complex and confusing, and we work to ensure the system is simple, get people the right information, and ensure they can get the right support when needed. Any adult living in Salisbury, including family and friends, can ask us how we could help. We provide guidance and information to help them find the support they need as easily as possible. All our services are aimed at helping people live their life as independently as possible in their community."

Phil Crocker had then asked Gillian Lye how she came to meet Mandy Howard.

"Mandy had learned there was a vacancy in the Housing Department, and she applied straightaway," said Gillian. "I don't know what pressures the HR people were under at the time, but Mandy reckoned the interview if you could call it that, was a ten-minute phone call between Salisbury and Merthyr. Because Mandy knew the job inside-out, they knew they were lucky to get her, and Mandy had to give notice to her boss that she was leaving almost as soon as she put the phone down."

"It was a bit of a rush then," said Bob Mears.

"I should say," said Gillian. "Mandy left home at six and rode her motorcycle across the Severn Bridge on the Monday morning when she was due to start work here. She arrived outside the council offices at half-past eight with a change of clothes and a wash kit in her panniers. I met her in the toilets at a quarter to nine when I arrived. She'd changed from her leathers into something suitable for the office and was brushing her hair. She asked me if I knew anyone with a spare room, as she hadn't had time to get anything sorted."

"Like I said, a bit of a rush," said Bob.

"I asked how she was going to manage, with only what she stood up in, plus her motorcycle leathers," said Gillian. "Mandy told me her father was taking her clothing and other personal items she wanted from her home to the railway station this morning. It would be a big help if someone had a car and could help retrieve the packages from Salisbury station tomorrow. I told her I would help and that I had a two-bedroomed bungalow on Hilltop Way. I'd only met her five minutes earlier, but she seemed nice enough."

"So, Mandy moved into your spare bedroom?" asked Bob Mears.

"She left her bike in the car park overnight, and I drove us home. Then, on our way to work in the morning, we dropped by the station to collect her belongings. It was a strange start, but I was right about her. She was a good person. Everyone will tell you the same. Mandy was good at her job, she never fell out with her colleagues, and although the Housing Department brought her into contact with a few residents that were, let's say, rough around the edges, she treated them fairly, and they recognised it."

"Had you always lived alone before Mandy moved from Merthyr?" asked Phil Crocker.

"I lived in the bungalow with Mother," said Gillian. "My father died from lung cancer in 1996, when he was just forty-eight. We lived near Old Sarum then and moved to the bungalow in 1998 because Mother couldn't manage the stairs due to her weight. She had a massive heart attack and died in 2006. So, I was a single girl, alone at thirty-two. When Mandy came to live with me, it was a godsend. The rent money was a bonus. It was the company I lacked most."

"What was the nature of your relationship?" asked Phil Crocker.

"We worked in the same group of buildings, and I'd like to believe we were friends," said Gillian. "I'm not sure what you're getting at."

"Were there boyfriends?" asked Bob.

Gus realised Phil Crocker and Bob Mears had the advantage of knowing what Gillian Lye looked like. He didn't know whether it was relevant. There were photos in the file of Mandy before she met her grisly end, and she left an impression.

Gus knew from experience nobody would have described Spider Crees as handsome, yet his appearance turned heads. Mandy wasn't a stunningly beautiful woman, but eyes are the window to the soul, and in every photo, she looked straight at the camera as if defying you to look away. Gus was beginning to appreciate what a couple they must have made.

"I've not been lucky with boyfriends," said Gillian.

Gus knew he only had to wait until Tuesday morning to see whether the reality matched the image in his head.

"What about Mandy?" asked Phil Crocker.

"She knew I wouldn't have approved of her bringing someone home," said Gillian. "Not that she ever did. Because I needed my car for home visits and couldn't guarantee when I'd be back at the Bourne Hill offices, Mandy rode her motorcycle to and from work. She stayed home in the evening during the week and went out at weekends.

Mandy told me she visited pubs and clubs around the city. We would share a bottle of wine here at home, but when she went out on her bike, the hard rock music she enjoyed determined which venue she went to. I never went with her. I was happier at home watching TV."

"How did you feel about her smoking in the house?" asked Phil Crocker.

"She didn't smoke while she was here. Mandy knew how I felt about cigarettes after my father died. I knew she smoked cannabis when she was out in the evenings."

"Did her use of cannabis increase during the time you lived together?" asked Bob.

"Hard to tell," said Gillian. "Maybe she cut back in the first few months, in case I objected and told her she needed to find another place. But, as I remember, once Mandy had settled here, her usage was regular but not excessive."

"Did she tell you when she met John Crees?" asked Bob Mears.

"Not straight away," said Gillian. "It was a Bank Holiday weekend, and one of the pubs had a series of groups appearing from nine to midnight from Friday to Monday. Mandy was out every night that weekend, and when we were watching TV together in the middle of the following week, she mentioned that she'd met someone. I didn't know the name when she told me, but I recognised his description. Once seen, never forgotten. I thought she was crazy, but it wasn't my place to tell her, so I held my tongue."

"Mandy didn't move out for a few months," said Phil Crocker. "Did Mandy being with Crees make things awkward between you?"

"Why should it?" said Gillian. "We carried on as we had before. We travelled to work separately, ate together in the evenings during the week, and watched TV if she wasn't seeing John. They did their own thing at weekends, mostly riding hundreds of miles together. But then, John asked Mandy to move into a house on Rampart Road. He came here on one occasion to help ferry her things to the house on their bikes."

"When did Mandy start working at the Winchester Gate pub?" asked Bob Mears.

"That was soon after she left Hilltop Way," said Gillian.

"Did you continue to speak to her after she moved out?" asked Phil Crocker.

"Of course, whenever our paths crossed at work. Which wasn't often, I suppose, but there was no animosity between us because she no longer needed a place to stay. I've got three cats now. One, I bought myself and two strays, so I'm not lonely most of the time. Weekends, when I'm not working, are the worst."

Gus wondered what Gillian was doing this weekend. Maybe her circumstances had altered in the past six years for her to have such a busy diary.

Something else was troubling him about the interview Phil Crocker and Bob Mears had conducted after the murder too, but for now, Gus decided to finish reading the report, and he'd discuss matters with Blessing on Monday after they'd spoken to Jeff Sheppard.

"Did you ever see John and Mandy together in Salisbury?" asked Phil Crocker.

"No, they didn't ride out this way," said Gillian. "My home visits are scattered around the city and the nearby villages. The narrow streets in the city, and country lanes, weren't where they wanted to be. Mandy told me they enjoyed the freedom of the wide-open roads of dual carriageways and motorways."

"When did you learn of their murder?" asked Bob Mears.

"I was in Laverstock that day," said Gillian. "I'd driven back into the city at three o'clock, and several people were in tears when I reached the office. My team leader told me what had happened. I decided to have a glass of wine we both enjoyed that night in Mandy's memory. I'm afraid I finished the bottle and cried myself to sleep."

Gus thought he heard a familiar sound. Suzie had arrived home.

"You didn't hang about then," she said as she burst through the front door. "I thought I might get home before you today."

Gus explained he'd preferred to study the murder file at home and had been reading for the past two hours.

"How did the rest of the day go?" asked Suzie.

"My boyish charm has earned me a lockable filing cabinet and an uneasy truce with Phil Crocker," said Gus. "I might have to keep an eye on Bob Mears, but overall it was a positive start. I had an interesting conversation with Mike Woodman, who was John Crees's employer. Mandy Howard's immediate boss was everything I expected a council employee to be, and I've scheduled an interview with the Police Surgeon first thing on Monday. On Tuesday, we'll chat to Mandy's landlady when she first arrived from South Wales."

"Not a long list, though, is it?" said Suzie as she sat beside him.

"I'm not sure how many of the bikers they interviewed after the murder will be worth pursuing," said Gus. "After we've spoken with Jeff Sheppard and Gillian Lye, we'll compile a new list using any new names they throw up. Mike Woodman told me John Crees was married before he left Basingstoke to join the Army. We can't rule that connection out without checking first. I admit there aren't many potential leads, but you never know."

"I know you," said Suzie. "You've got a niggle, haven't you? Do you want to share?"

"It was something someone said to me today," said Gus. "It didn't fit with what I knew about the case, but whether it was important or not, I can't say."

" I'm going to shower, change, and get ready to visit the supermarket," said Suzie. "What do you need to do?"

"The same," said Gus. "I don't suppose…?"

"Do you remember that duo, Sparks?" said Suzie.

"Ron and Russell Mael," said Gus.

"Our shower ain't big enough for the both of us," said Suzie.

## Saturday, 1 December 2018

GUS WAS awake at half-past seven. Nothing had come to him during the night. He'd had no sudden lightbulb moment that illuminated the dark corner of his mind where that odd comment was hidden.

He knew the more he tried to identify it, the harder it would be to find it. So, he got up and walked to the kitchen. Suzie joined him ten minutes later.

"What's for breakfast?" she asked.

"We've got so many options after our weekly shop, I couldn't decide," said Gus. "Then, I remembered we're visiting your parents. We might just as well have coffee and toast before we leave. There's no way Jackie will let us leave without knocking up a full-English."

"You're not often wrong," said Suzie, " but you're right again. Thank goodness I grabbed a jar of Nutella spread last night."

"Yuk. Not for me," said Gus. "I've got a jar of marmalade in the fridge. It's been open a while, but it's a safer bet."

They were pleasantly surprised when they ventured outside at a quarter to ten.

"That biting cold wind has eased," said Suzie. "It feels warmer this morning."

"Those clouds hovering near the top of the hill remind me of something Bert Penman told me the first winter I moved here," said Gus. "After several days of bitter cold and icy fingers everywhere, winter lulls you into a false sense of security. Those are snow clouds."

"Oh, lovely," said Suzie. "Do you think we'll have a white Christmas?"

"Well, as this is England, if we get snow in the next twenty-four hours, it will be gone as quickly as it arrived."

"The country will still grind to a halt," said Suzie.

Gus couldn't argue with that statement. He drove them to Worton Farm as a watery sun broke through the clouds. Fifteen minutes later, he parked the Focus outside.

John Ferris came striding across the farmyard to hug his daughter.

"Good to see you are looking so well, darling," he said. "You too, Gus."

John led them inside, and true to form, Jackie was busy in the kitchen.

"How's everyone?" asked Suzie.

"We're fine," said Jackie. "Grace and Blessing will be down in a tick. The smell of fresh bread encourages them to stir their stumps, and once they've opened both eyes, I start making breakfast. Have you eaten already?"

Gus smiled at Suzie.

"Just a bite, Mum," said Suzie. "Don't go overboard. Anyway, Grace doesn't do fry-ups. What a vegan all-English looks like, I dread to think."

"Seitan sausages, scrambled tofu, and tempeh bacon, with cherry tomatoes, baked beans, and mushrooms," said Jackie. "Although, it's not a regular meal for them. The girls have needed something warming to fortify them against the cold these past few days. They found life in the countryside a bit different away from their desks in a warm office. I made extra helpings of hot broth for them to take in their thermos flasks."

"How are things in the village, Gus?" asked John while Jackie and Suzie chatted on the other side of the kitchen.

"Much the same, John," said Gus. "I've only spent a couple of hours on the allotment, and my old friend, Bert, hasn't been there. He's getting over the flu. One bit of news you might be interested in. Our vicar is getting married on Christmas Eve to Brett Penman, the vet."

"I know him," said John. "Brett took a look at my horses a month or two back. He's based in Wootton Bassett, isn't he?"

"Yes, and he's Bert's grandson, as you know. The Reverend and Brett decided to tie the knot earlier than planned."

"I understand," said John. "Older relatives are keen to see their kids settled before they pass."

"I'm not sure whether that was a subtle hint or a veiled threat," said Gus.

"I'm like you, Gus. I don't consider myself older," said John. "As long as Suzie's happy, I'm not bothered whether she wants me to walk her down the aisle. Jackie might appreciate the opportunity for a new outfit and a fancy hat, though."

"The christening will provide an occasion worth dressing up for," said Gus.

Grace Packenham appeared at the bottom of the stairs.

"Hello, Gus. What a surprise. Did you remember to ask everyone about Friday night?"

"I ticked all the boxes I could tick, Grace," said Gus. "I didn't spend long enough at London Road to catch Divya Yadav, but we still have time. How was Farm Watch?"

"I hadn't realised there were so many farms in the county," said Grace. "We've only scratched the surface. Blessing found it a challenge. Cows, horses, pigs, ducks, and chickens seemed to gravitate toward her wherever we went."

"CRT's version of St Francis of Assisi," said Gus.

"Even though most of the animals were friendly, Blessing wasn't happy."

Blessing Umeh soon joined them, wearing a thick, chunky jumper and denim jeans.

"Straight off the cover of Horse and Hound," said Suzie. "What happened to the shy girl from Royal Leamington Spa?"

"It's cold," said Blessing. "I heard what Grace was saying. Our focus was supposed to be protecting the bigger equipment farmers use daily. Instead, I spent more time shooing animals away. It was fun at times, though. Do you have any news for us, guv?"

"It's Gus when we're not at work, Blessing," said Gus. "Has DS Mercer told you what's happening on Monday?"

"I'm going to Salisbury with you, aren't I?" said Blessing. "Why only the two of us?"

Gus quickly explained what had happened during the week while Jackie dished up two styles of fried breakfast.

"I don't know how you do it, Jackie," said Gus.

"I cut my teeth multi-tasking for the whims of three teenage kids, and their food loves and hates," said Jackie. "Once you've all had your fill and got out from under my feet, I can start baking."

"It's much appreciated, Jackie," said Grace.

"And tasty," said Blessing.

"Do you girls have plans for today?" asked Jackie.

"I'm driving into Devizes, looking for clothes," said Grace. "Bigger clothes."

"Jamie's picking me up at two," said Blessing. "What's on the menu for Monday, guv?"

"A meeting with the Police Surgeon as soon as we arrive at Bourne Hill," said Gus. "If you can spare five minutes, I'll run through my questions for him."

"OK," said Blessing. "Can we use the parlour, please, John?"

"Be my guest," said John. "I haven't lit the fire yet, but it's the oldest part of the farmhouse, and the walls are twice as thick as anywhere else. So you won't freeze."

Gus and Blessing slipped into the next room.

"I hadn't realised I was expected to supervise the Farm Watch initiative, Suzie," said Grace.

"No doubt you coped, Grace," said Suzie. "The female PCSOs won't have to keep an eye out for wandering hands now DI Wallis is out of the frame."

"What a creep," said Grace. "Has Gus told you what's happening with the others next week?"

"Lydia, Alex, and Neil will be at Gablecross," said Suzie. "Unless Melody changes arrangements. You'll get the chance to catch up with everyone on Friday night."

"I can't wait to get back to the office and get stuck into this new case Gus and Blessing are tackling," said Grace. "Although, I can't say I'm looking forward to sharing the space with another group of people."

"You'll get on with Sarah Holland, alright," said Suzie. "You're much the same age, and Sarah and I have known one another for years."

"I hope I get to join Gus at Bourne Hill before he wraps up the case."

"He's only just started to look at it, Grace," said Suzie.

"Blessing and Gus will be interviewing people in a nice warm office at Bourne Hill while I'll be chasing PCSO and uniforms across Salisbury Plain, making sure they're not slacking."

"Gus thinks the clouds we saw this morning could mean snow," said Suzie.

"Just when I thought my day couldn't get any worse," said Grace.

Gus and Blessing returned from the parlour. He was waving his car keys, which suggested he was ready to drive them home. The threat of a dusting of snow wouldn't stop him from spending what was left of the daylight on his allotment.

Suzie and Gus said goodbye to everyone and were soon motoring home to Urchfont.

"A light meal tonight, I think," said Gus. "Wherever we decide to eat."

Sunday was a day or rest. There was snow on high ground, which included Alton Barnes, the highest point in the county, but Urchfont didn't receive enough to make a decent-sized snowball.

## *Monday, 3 December 2018*

GUS LEFT HOME before Suzie again. He needed to get to Worton before twenty-past eight if they wanted to get to Bourne Hill by nine. The skies were still cloudy, but they held sleet and rain rather than snow.

Blessing Umeh came bustling out of the farmhouse kitchen door. She was dressed for the office but clutched her thermos flask to her bosom. She got into the passenger seat and closed the door.

"Hot broth?" asked Gus.

"Coffee," said Blessing. "I know what our Gaggia can provide, but Bourne Hill is an unknown quantity. It's black, so you can have some if you can find a clean cup."

"Did you have a good weekend?" asked Gus.

"Jamie took me to meet his parents," said Blessing. "They live in Guildford, in a lovely house."

"You've done the rounds now," said Gus. "Jamie has met Kelechi and Maryam already."

"Yes," said Blessing, but she wasn't prepared to continue with Gus's line of questioning.

Gus slowed as they went through Shrewton, but the glass debris had been removed, and traffic flowed with worrying ease. He parked the Focus in the visitor's car park at five to nine.

"We'll pop upstairs to let you see where we'll be working," said Gus. "Then we'll walk to Holmwood House. Don't worry. It's only ten minutes door to door."

They reached the first-floor office, and Gus pointed out the cubicle.

"A desk, two chairs, and a tiny filing cabinet," said Blessing. "What a comedown."

"It's only temporary, Blessing," said Gus. "You can lock your thermos flask in the cabinet. Here's a key. Attach it to your set of keys, and don't let it out of your sight."

Blessing giggled.

"You're funny, guv. Surely, we can trust our fellow officers?"

"While hiding your thermos, you can return this file folder to the bottom drawer."

Blessing carried the two items to the cubicle, secured them, and returned to join Gus. She was still giggling.

They walked down Greencroft Street, turned left onto Milford Hill, and crossed the street to Fowler's Road. As they walked into the foyer of Holmwood House, Blessing's watch read thirteen minutes past nine.

Gus explained who they were to the member of staff who approached them, and two minutes later, they were shown into Jeff Sheppard's room.

"Good morning, Jeff," said Gus. "It's been a while. Do you remember me?"

"Of course I do, Gus. I'm not senile," said Jeff. "Who have you got with you?"

"DC Blessing Umeh, sir," said Blessing.

"Nigerian, am I right?" said Jeff.

"Born and bred in Warwickshire, sir," said Blessing. "But my parents came from Nigeria."

"I hope you're listening to every word this man tells you, DC Umeh," said Jeff. "There were only a couple of detectives I could stand hovering by my shoulder at a crime scene, and Gus Freeman was one of them. He knew when to keep quiet and which questions to ask when it was appropriate for him to speak."

"We're all learning as much from Mr Freeman as possible, sir," said Blessing.

"Right, my tai chi lesson starts in just over an hour. What do you want to know?"

"I have a couple of questions that weren't asked of you at the time, Jeff," said Gus. "Do you think the killer brought the murder weapon with them, or did they use a hammer that was to hand? They could have found it in the house, or the garden shed. The second question is, who was struck first; John Crees or Mandy Howard?"

"If we'd known the intended target, we might have assumed they were the first person struck," said Jeff. "However, both parties could feasibly have been the intended target. The detectives never answered that question. I don't believe the killer was invited into the house, even if they were known to the couple. It's most likely they were battered to death in their sleep. Neighbours heard no screams or sounds of a struggle. If Crees had been awake when the first blow was struck, whoever the recipient was, he would have fought back. I found no defensive wounds that suggested he'd been allowed to do that. His body was found sprawled across the bed, lying across Mandy Howard. That could have occurred when he fell after getting struck for a second or third time."

"You don't believe the attack started downstairs?" said Gus.

"There were no signs of any attack on the ground floor," said Jeff. "No, the simplest explanation is that the killer forced entry through the kitchen door and made his way to the bedroom. I believe the killer knew the couple well; they were familiar with their movements and knew Mandy Howard wouldn't be home until midnight. They would also have expected John Crees to collect her from the Winchester Gate pub and walk her home."

"As soon as John Crees left to collect Mandy, the killer

took advantage of the empty house and broke the window pane," said Blessing. "When the couple returned, they went straight to bed, and the killer moved from his hiding place. Once he was sure they were asleep, he crept upstairs and attacked them."

"Very good, DC Umeh," said Jeff. "Your method has its merits, but either John or Mandy might have gone into the kitchen to fetch a glass of water or make a hot drink. They would have seen the broken glass by the door."

"Perhaps they did follow the couple from the pub," said Blessing. "Despite it being riskier to break the window pane while they were in the house."

"Whichever way that first step occurred, it's plain it was a planned attack," said Gus. "No way was it a robbery gone wrong."

"I agree, Gus," said Jeff Sheppard. "Did Crocker and Mears ever consider the motive for the attack to be jealousy?"

"John Crees had been married," said Gus. "But he was divorced long before he moved to Salisbury. Mandy Howard was never married. I've talked to three people who knew the couple, and while they lived in Salisbury, there were no significant relationships for either of them. I'm sure, if there had been, Phil Crocker and Bob Mears would have followed that thread."

"There were no eye witnesses who saw anyone fleeing the scene," said Jeff. "I couldn't determine whether the killer was male or female. Don't frown like that, DC Umeh. A young woman like you could inflict terrible damage with a four-pound lump hammer. I beg you not to try to count the number of blows each victim suffered. The scene that greeted me when I stepped into that bedroom was worse than anything I've seen."

"The level of overkill did suggest a crime of passion," said Gus. "Yet, despite all the interviews they carried out, Crocker and Mears had no physical description of any suspects. The killer didn't leave behind any forensic evidence."

"It was a mystery six years ago, Gus," said Jeff Sheppard. "I can't see it will be any easier to unravel this time around. Was there anything else?"

"Not this morning, Jeff," said Gus. "We know where you are if we think you can help."

"Good to meet you, Dr Sheppard," said Blessing.

"You too, DC Umeh," said Jeff Sheppard. He stood up slowly and followed them to the door. "Good hunting."

Gus and Blessing were soon outside on the pavement and returning to Bourne Hill.

"We didn't make much progress there, guv," said Blessing. "Or did I miss something?"

"We lost nothing by getting Jeff Sheppard to express his feelings about the murder. They aligned with the reports in the file, except for the jealousy aspect. That was different. Maybe after six years, Jeff's seeing something that wasn't there, or perhaps he sensed it as he stood over the bodies but didn't convey those thoughts to DCI Crocker. I'll ask Phil when we get back."

"There's more activity here than when we left, guv," said Blessing as they approached the front door of the building. A couple of cars were just leaving, followed by a van.

As Gus and Blessing crossed the office to their cubicle, Phil Crocker hurried towards them.

"I presume this is your colleague, Gus," said Phil. "Pleased to meet you, detective. Sorry, I can't stop. A suspicious death's been reported out at Hilltop Way."

## Chapter Nine

"WHAT'S UP, GUV?" asked Blessing.

"Hilltop Way is where Gillian Lye lives," said Gus. "She's our first appointment tomorrow morning."

"If we were in the Old Police Station office. We'd have a map of Salisbury on the wall by now," said Blessing. "I have no idea where that address is. There could be twenty houses on Hilltop Way or two hundred. So the sudden death could be unrelated."

Gus suspected the clouds he'd seen at the weekend had less to do with an impending snowstorm and more with a nightmare.

"Does Bob Mears still team up with the DCI, guv?" asked Blessing. "Why was a Detective Chief Inspector needed at the scene, anyway?"

"Thanks for reminding me, Blessing," said Gus. "Just as well that one of us is thinking straight. Since Phil Crocker *is* attending the incident, it adds weight to my fear that this suspicious death is connected to our cold case. I read the report on the interview DI Crocker and DS Mears conducted with Mandy Howard's landlady in 2012 when I got home on Friday afternoon."

"How do we find out what's going on, guv?" asked Blessing.

"We'd get shot down in flames if we drove out to Hilltop Way to take a look," said Gus. "I'm not very good at sitting on my hands, waiting. We could update our digital files if we could access our usual kit. I've been taking notes and recording conversations on my phone where I felt it necessary, but I'd like to get things into a file before I forget something that could prove important."

"I brought my laptop with me, just in case," said Blessing. "Let me have a word with the detective in the next cubicle. I'll get the wi-fi password and ask how to access other systems we might need. We can send the files to your computer in the CRT office and get our ducks in a row when we're there next. I can contact Divya Yadav in the Hub to get her help as and when we need it. Why don't you see if you can find DS Mears? He could give you more detail on who made the emergency call and when."

Gus nodded and walked across the office to find Bob Mears.

Bob sat at his desk, almost hidden by the files piled on either side of his computer screen.

"Hilltop Way, Bob," said Gus. "Is that out towards Old Sarum and Ford? I can't remember visiting an address in that area during my time here."

"It's a couple of miles from here," said Bob. "Right on the edge of Castle Hill Country Park. The A345 takes you direct to Old Sarum, and the houses on Hilltop Way are on the right. Why?"

"Phil's just left in a hurry. He told me there had been a report of a suspicious death."

"First I've heard of it," said Bob. "We're not joined at the hip like when you worked here, Gus."

"Who'd most likely get assigned to the case?" asked Gus.

Bob stood up, walked to the edge of his cubicle, and checked for heads around the office.

"Chris Stanton and Noah Baker aren't home," he said. "Chris is Phil's blue-eyed boy these days. So, DI Stanton and DS Baker will determine whether the death is more than suspicious."

"If Hilltop Way runs along the edge of the Country Park, we're talking fifty properties on either side of the road maximum, are we?"

"No, most properties are on the left-hand side with an unrestricted view of the parkland. There's a crescent at the far end, where planners have relaxed the restrictions, and a few properties have been built on the right. I read in the Journal the other day that a developer has submitted an application for ten more semi-detached bungalows," said Bob. "I don't exactly where that plot is, but they would take the number closer to the hundred. There's a mix of housing on Hilltop Way, two-bed bungalows, up to four, or even five-bedroom houses. What's Phil doing up there, anyway? He's usually tied up in meetings."

"Where did you interview Gillian Lye?" asked Gus. "The young woman who took Mandy Howard in as a lodger when she moved from Merthyr."

"She came here," said Bob. "It was only a short walk from the council office. Why?"

"Gillian Lye lives on Hilltop Way," said Gus. "I spoke to her on Friday afternoon, just before she finished work. She told me she was busy this weekend and today, so we arranged to meet at her home at ten tomorrow morning."

"What, you think Phil's tagged along with Stanton and Baker because someone connected to the Crees and Howard case has been found dead?"

"I realise we don't know the deceased's identity," said Gus. "Also, it could turn out to be natural causes."

"Both Gillian Lye's parents died young, as I remember," said Bob. "Her mother was grossly overweight, and her heart gave out. After walking a short distance from the offices on the other side of the car park, the daughter was out of breath. Gillian Lye took after her mother."

"I did wonder," said Gus. "Although Mandy Howard socialised, particularly at weekends, Gillian never accompanied her. She seemed happiest sitting at home watching TV with a glass of wine."

"Gillian filled in several blanks we had in Mandy's life between leaving home and moving in with Spider Crees," said Bob. "It was useful background, but once Crees and Howard became a couple, Gillian Lye barely saw her former lodger."

"We both know you and Phil couldn't solve this case in 2012," said Gus. "Either you missed something or misinterpreted what you learned. Is it possible there was a third reason?"

"What? Someone was manipulating the information we got to see?" said Bob. "Blimey, that's a stretch. What is it they say? A conspiracy's alive and well and living in Salisbury. Who could have done that, another copper?"

"I haven't mentioned this to Phil yet, " said Gus, "but since I arrived here last Friday morning, someone told me something I realised might be important. The idea flashed through my brain while I listened to Phil tell me about how you had approached the case."

"Now you can't quite connect the two comments," said Bob. "That happens to me a lot. Far more these days than when I was a young Detective Constable."

"Bob Martin will be working downstairs for another hour or two," said Gus. "I think I'll pop down to see whether he took the emergency call and if he's had an update from Hilltop Way."

"If I were a betting man," said Bob Mears, "and it *was* Gillian Lye, I reckon she keeled over like her mother and was dead before she hit the ground. The Police Surgeon will have left within five minutes of Phil Crocker's arrival. Nothing to see here. Please move on."

"We spoke with Jeff Sheppard earlier," said Gus. "He's still as bright as a button. So who's your latest Police Surgeon?"

"Catherine Gumm," said Bob Mears. "Queen Victoria is her nickname. Although, I don't think a smile has cracked her face since birth. It's not the result of losing a husband. Ms Gumm knows her stuff, doesn't suffer fools gladly, if at all, and threatens to remain in Salisbury until she retires."

"How old is she, Bob?" asked Gus.

"Twenty-eight," he muttered.

"Ouch," said Gus.

He left Bob Mears with his file mountain and headed downstairs to Reception.

"Hello again, Gus," said Bob. "What's occurring?"

"Phil Crocker shot out of here earlier on his way to Hilltop Way. Did you take the emergency call that started the stampede?"

Bob referred to the logbook in front of him.

"It's an odd one. The first call came in at nine-fifty-five

from Daisy Field. She's a manager in the Adult Care Department just across the car park. You can't blame her parents for the name; Daisy married a chap called Field. Anyway, Mrs Field wanted to report a missing person. I asked who was missing and for how long. Mrs Field told me her colleague, Gillian Lye, had attended a weekend residential conference near Swindon. Gillian had signed in at ten on Saturday morning and had been booked into a room at the venue for Saturday night. The conference ended with a dinner on Sunday evening, and Gillian signed out at nine-thirty. Her car was caught on the venue's CCTV leaving the car park at nine forty-one pm. I've heard it's a blurry picture, but the conference organiser was happy Gillian Lye was the driver, and she was alone."

"Why would anyone report her missing?" asked Gus. "It's only fifteen hours since she was last seen alive."

"Daisy Field told me Gillian had called her last night at six, just before she went down to dinner, to book a half day's holiday tomorrow morning. She was already off work today because she had a hospital appointment. Gillian was due at the New Hall Hospital, near Bodenham. They're a private concern dealing with patients like Gillian Lye. She was clinically obese and was considering which surgical option she preferred."

"So, she missed her appointment," said Gus. "That's not uncommon, and none of the surgical options available to her would have been a walk in the park. She's probably parked a few miles up the road, trying to pluck up the courage to go through with it."

"You're forgetting Vic Millar," said Bob Martin.

"Who's he?" asked Gus.

"He's Gillian's next-door neighbour," said Bob. "Vic was convinced that although Gillian's car wasn't in the carport, she was inside the house. Because, when he was getting ready for bed last night, Mr Millar saw headlights swinging into her driveway at a quarter to eleven. That ties in with how long Gillian would have taken to drive home. Vic Millar's bed is against the adjoining wall, and he's often complained to Ms Lye that her television is so loud it keeps him awake."

"How did Vic Millar get involved?" asked Gus.

"After she'd called me, Mrs Field drove to Hilltop Way to check on Gillian in case she had been taken ill. She wasn't answering her home phone or her mobile." Bob explained. "Vic Millar came out of his front door to ask if he could help. When Mrs Field explained who she was and was concerned about Gillian, Mr Millar told her he'd heard dreadful noises coming from next door at about eleven last night. He'd hammered on the wall, hoping Gillian would turn down the volume on whatever she was watching, and within minutes it was quiet enough for him to drop off to sleep. The last thing he remembered was the sound of a car pulling away, but he didn't see any headlights."

"So that prompted Daisy Field to dial 999 for the second time," said Gus.

"I sent a police constable and a PCSO to the address," said Bob. "Vic Millar and Daisy Field were waiting on the front doorstep. As soon as our people got out of the car, a lady from a house further along the road came running up the pavement, waving a key. She told them her name was Anna Phillips, and she'd agreed to feed Gillian Lye's cats while she was away. She was waiting to see Gillian's car on the drive before returning the key. The constable took the key, opened the front door, stepped inside, and called out. There was no reply, and the PCSO followed the young lad inside. They found Gillian Lye on the floor in the front room. There was no blood or obvious signs of how she'd died. They secured the scene, made the necessary call, and sent Vic Millar and Anna Phillips home, reminding them that detectives would call on them later."

"No wonder Phil Crocker rushed to Hilltop Way," said Gus. "As soon as he heard the dead person's name, he thought it might be connected to his six-year-old murder case."

"What? The case you've reopened?" asked Bob. "Have you thought through what you're saying?"

"Not entirely, Bob," said Gus. "I'd better get upstairs and wait for the balloon to go up."

When he reached the cubicle, Blessing was busy on her laptop. A street map of Salisbury and the surrounding district was blu-tacked to the back wall.

"We're all set, guv," she said. "Apart from having open discussions with the rest of the team, it's just like sitting in the office. So what did you find out?"

Gus told her what Bob Mears and Bob Martin had told him.

"I don't know enough about the original case to give a credible explanation, guv," said Blessing. "It sounds like you're saying someone was waiting for Gillian Lye when she returned home from her weekend conference. The noises the next-door neighbour heard could have been Gillian being attacked. There was no blood, so perhaps she was strangled. Unless they knew what they were looking for, a young constable and a PCSO might miss signs of strangulation on the body of a large woman like Gillian. They would know not to move the body and leave everything as they found it for the Police Surgeon to examine more closely."

"I can't argue with your thought process, Blessing," said Gus. "The car being moved just after eleven, without lights, suggests the intruder took advantage of a free ride home on a cold night. Uniforms will be searching for Gillian's car as we speak. They will know their best chance of spotting it is to look for a trail of smoke."

"If the intruder stole Gillian's car, does that mean they walked to Hilltop Way?" said Blessing. "Couldn't it be a burglary gone wrong, guv? Someone saw the place in darkness, broke in, and was disturbed when she drove onto the drive. Gillian could have had a heart attack; the intruder panicked, grabbed her keys, and escaped in the car."

"Uniforms didn't report any signs of a break-in," said Gus. "No, it sounds more plausible the intruder arrived on foot and lay in wait."

"Well, that suggests the intruder knew Gillian was away for the weekend and would be home between ten-thirty and eleven. It was too cold to hang around on the off chance she'd drive home sometime Sunday evening. So that means they knew Gillian well and knew her movements."

"That phrase sounds familiar, doesn't it?" said Gus. "But it gets worse. If it *was* murder, or even if they scared her so much she suffered a massive heart attack, it means Gillian Lye had to be prevented from meeting with us tomorrow morning."

"She knew something that could have helped you solve the John Crees and Mandy Howard murder," said Blessing. "I see what you mean by familiar, guv. That was what Dr Sheppard said - he believed the killer knew the couple well; they were familiar with their movements. Is it possible that the killer has struck again?"

Gus sat in the vacant chair. He needed to think. How would anyone know they were due to speak to Gillian Lye tomorrow morning? He'd called her just before she left the office. Gillian had told Anna Phillips she would be away until Sunday evening. To suggest the neighbours were involved was ludicrous. But who else was there? Daisy Field had taken a call from Gillian from the conference venue at six on Sunday evening. Was that call from Gillian's mobile or a phone at the venue? Besides the car being taken, the uniforms hadn't found evidence of a robbery. Did the intruder grab Gillian's car keys and leave? Or did they take her handbag and purse too?

"A penny for them, guv," said Blessing.

"I can't make sense of it, Blessing," said Gus.

"Tell you what, guv," said Blessing. "The detective next door had a spare cup. I'll give it a good wash before you use it. He told me there's no objection to bringing food into the office, provided it's not likely to stink the place out. He recommended a decent deli which is a two-minute walk away. So I'll pop out and get us lunch, and you can start adding your information to the file I've set up. Typing the contents of your notebook into the laptop might help with that snippet of information you thought was important. Its relevance might come to you."

"You're a star, Blessing," said Gus. "Any chance you could wash that cup before you leave so I can have a coffee while I type?"

Gus was checking through his notebook five minutes later, sipping a black coffee, and Blessing was waiting to be served in the deli. He heard a knock on the partition. Phil Crocker had returned.

"Sorry about this, Gus," said Phil. "Where's your colleague?"

"She's buying lunch," said Gus.

"You've got her well-trained," said Phil. "Look, we've got a problem."

"Bob Martin gave me the lowdown on events leading to

you and your number one detective team rushing to Hilltop Way. Gillian Lye is dead, isn't she?"

"That's the problem," said Phil. He sat in the vacant chair.

"Has Catherine Gumm given any indication of the cause of death?" asked Gus.

"Gillian Lye was punched in the face and then strangled," said Phil. "An eyewitness told uniforms Gillian returned home in her car at around ten forty-five."

"Yes, and then Vic Millar heard a car drive away soon after," said Gus. "So, as there were no signs of a break-in, DI Stanton believes Gillian opened the front door and went inside. She had enough time to chat with her cats and heard a knock at the door. Perhaps she thought Anna Phillips was returning her spare key, despite the hour. Gillian answered the door. Her attacker thumped her in the face, shoved her into the lounge, and choked her to death. Nothing else fits the timeline."

"Catherine Gumm couldn't argue with the facts," said Phil. "Death occurred within fifteen minutes of Gillian Lye getting home. The autopsy can't occur until Thursday, but we don't expect any surprises. Forensics are still at the scene and will be for the remainder of the day. Chris Stanton and Noah Baker are talking to Vic Millar and Anna Phillips. When they finish there, they'll visit Daisy Field. On my way into the building, I just heard that a burnt-out car matching the description of the one owned by Gillian Lye has been found near Ford, on the far side of the Castle Hill Country Park."

"Are uniforms carrying out a house-to-house on Hilltop Way?" asked Gus.

"That's standard procedure," said Phil. "Although, we

already believe we've spoken to the main players. Gillian wasn't good at making friends."

Blessing Umeh appeared at the doorway, and the smell of hot pasties filled the cubicle.

"I'll give you two fifteen minutes to finish your lunch," said Phil. "There are things I need to do. Can I see you both in my office when you're ready?"

"Of course," said Gus. "There's something Stanton and Baker need to do, and quickly."

Phil Crocker shook his head and left them alone.

"Your worst fears were realised then, guv?" said Blessing. "Gillian Lye was murdered."

"Yes, and I didn't spend long enough on my notebook to identify that potential lead we could follow. Phil's first comment when he walked in was that we had a problem. I think he meant us. So let's have that pasty; at least we'll hear the bad news on a full stomach."

Blessing poured herself a coffee from her thermos flask and topped up Gus's cup.

Fifteen minutes later, Gus finished the last of his coffee and looked in vain for a waste bin to get rid of the wrapper from the deli. He wiped his mouth with the back of his hand.

"Come on, Blessing, let's get it over with."

Phil Crocker was on the phone when they reached his office. He waved at the spare chairs on the outside wall. Gus and Blessing brought them to his desk, sat, and waited. When Gus heard Geoff's name, he knew their time here was up.

"You probably heard some of that, Gus," said Phil after he ended the call. "I've spoken to DS Mercer at London Road. He's agreed that you and DC Umeh can't be involved in an ongoing murder investigation. By the end of today, you must hand over everything you've learned in the interviews you've undertaken. Stanton and Baker will start with a blank canvas and build a picture of Gillian Lye's life, looking for possible suspects. Early signs indicate robbery wasn't the motive for the attack, but Chris Stanton wants to rule out every other possibility before linking her death to that of John Crees and Mandy Howard."

"I haven't finished updating my files yet, sir," said Gus. "Do we stay here or return to the Old Police Station office?"

"Geoff Mercer said you should return to the office, get to know your new residents, and await further instructions. He mentioned Farm Watch as a possibility for DC Umeh. How long do you need to get the details of your interviews and impressions into shape to hand over to Chris Stanton?"

"Several hours, sir," said Gus, crossing his fingers in his lap.

"The end of the day then," said Phil.

"Can I ask a question, sir?" asked Blessing.

"Of course," said Phil.

"Did the killer take anything besides the car keys with them when they left the house?"

"Yes, the victim's mobile phone was missing. According to her boss, Daisy Field, she carried it in her handbag. A large bag was found beside the body, and various items, including her purse, had been scattered on the floor. Money and credit cards in the purse were untouched. Chris Stanton told me the forensic team leader thought the random nature of the items and how they were discarded suggested the killer was searching for something."

"That goes without saying," said Gus.

"Why?" asked Phil Crocker. "Gillian Lye could have opened the handbag when she entered the house, dropped a couple of items on the floor when she jumped up to answer the door, and then the bag got kicked around during the ensuing struggle."

"You need to get a forensic team to the council offices to check Gillian's desk phone for a bug, sir," said Gus. "Ask the guys at Hilltop Way to check her home phone too. It's the only explanation for the killer knowing when Gillian would get home. She had to die before we went to talk to her in the morning."

"Are you serious?" asked Phil.

"Deadly serious," said Gus. "Look, I can't say I'm happy about getting dragged off the case, but I appreciate how DI Stanton and DS Baker feel. They don't want me sitting on their shoulder, tutting at every move they make. However, after forty years in the game, I know Gillian's death is linked to the cold case, and we're dealing with someone who will stop at nothing to cover their tracks. They either knew Gillian Lye could reveal something that would help us or couldn't take the risk; she might put two and two together and realise who the killer was, even after six years. It happens all the time. A witness goes over past events, and although they believe they've told detectives every detail, over and over, and there's nothing left to tell, suddenly, they recall something trivial. They'll say *Person A left the house at eight-thirty, and he was wearing a raincoat. Although, why he was wearing a scarf in September, I can't imagine.* We pick up that new piece of the jigsaw, which gives us a better picture of what really happened."

"We'll look stupid if we find nothing suspicious at the council office," said Phil.

"There would be an even bigger outcry if another person connected to the case were murdered before we get to speak with them," said Gus.

"Who might be at risk, guv?" asked Blessing.

"I wish I could answer that, Blessing," sighed Gus. "Suzie remarked that our interview list was lacking in depth. But it didn't seem worth talking to two dozen bikers who rode past DI Crocker's front door six years ago, so I thought the main players were Jeff Sheppard, Mike Woodman, Emily Farrell, and Gillian Lye."

"Emily and Gillian worked in different departments, guv," said Blessing.

"If we check Gillian's phone, we should check Emily's, too," said Gus. "We've spoken to her already, but the killer couldn't have been alerted by a phone call on that occasion. I walked across the car park, followed the signs to the Housing Department, and sat with her at her desk."

"Did Ms Farrell tell you anything new?" asked Phil Crocker.

"Emily gave us valuable background on the character of John Crees and her colleague, Mandy Howard. There were no major discrepancies between Emily's version of events and those in the file. I haven't transcribed that interview yet, so something she said might work loose and explain that niggle I've been suffering."

The detective from the office next to their cubicle tapped on Phil Crocker's door.

"Excuse me, sir. I've just answered the phone on Mr Freeman's desk. Sergeant Martin has a message for him handed in at Reception."

"I'll pop down to collect it, guv," said Blessing.

"That could prove interesting," said Gus. "The only person I asked to tell me if they remembered anything, no matter how insignificant it might seem, and to give it to Bob, was Emily Farrell."

"Chris Stanton will still insist you pack your bags, and

let him get on with what he's paid to do, Gus," said Phil Crocker. "He kept reminding me at Hilltop Way you were a mere consultant, and in the unlikely event he needed to consult you, he could always get your number."

"I can't wait to meet him," said Gus. "What's his success rate?"

"Impressive," said Phil. "Noah Baker hasn't been paired with him for long. Chris was partnered with the DS involved in that Novichok business earlier in the year."

"I couldn't believe something like that could happen here," said Gus.

He'd watched the news and read the papers back in March when former Russian spy Sergei Skripal, and his daughter Yulia, were found unconscious on a park bench, and trails of the nerve agent were located in the city. Salisbury then became embroiled in a national emergency and an international crisis. The Russian couple weren't the only victims of the attack. Gus had heard a detective, who came into contact with the poison at the Skripal's home, had been hospitalised but luckily survived.

"So, Noah Baker took over from DS Bailey," said Gus. "Has he returned to work?"

"I don't think he'll ever be the same again," said Phil. "He's not alone, of course."

At the end of June, two members of the public had also fallen ill. Tragically, one died in Salisbury District Hospital in July. The nerve agent attack was attributed to the Russians. Two dozen Russian diplomats were expelled, and the PM called the incident an unlawful use of force by the Russian state against the UK.

"Do you think the CPS will ever gather sufficient evidence to charge anyone?" asked Gus.

"The Met Police were drafted in to oversee the investigation," said Phil. "It was considered too big an operation for us to handle. A pair of GRU military intelligence service agents could get charged with offences, including conspiracy to murder over the attack. The Russians insist there was nothing criminal about two Russians seen in Salisbury before the attack. Moscow said they were on holiday."

"Well, they would, wouldn't they?" said Gus.

"The Ministry of Defence is carrying out a clean-up of twelve sites around the city," said Phil Crocker. "It could be a year before they can declare the city completely free of decontamination. However, the Government has promised money to aid recovery, boost tourism, and support businesses forced to close for a considerable period. For example, the restaurant where the couple ate before falling reopened only a month ago. The Novichok incident will impact some members of our community for ever, but for eight hundred years, Salisbury has shown how resilient this city can be, and in times of crisis, it pulls together. That's why I love living and working here."

Blessing returned from Reception with a hand written note.

"This is what you were waiting for, guv," she said.

She opened the sheet of paper and showed it to Gus and Phil Crocker.

*Mr Freeman,*

*You were right. I did remember something odd that happened. It was when we were moving into one of the offices previously occupied by the police. An engineer came in to sort out the phones. I could tell at once that Mandy knew him and that she clearly didn't like him.*

*They didn't speak, but the guy was creepy. We were so busy with the move and getting things ready to start work the following Monday that I never asked her who he was. He was much the same age as Mandy,*

*tall, tanned, had long hair, and wore a black t-shirt with the company*
*logo, black jeans, and trainers. I've not seen him since.*
*I don't know if this will help,*
*Emily Farrell*

"You don't need to ask twice, Gus," said Phil Crocker. "We didn't hear that before. I'll get a sweep done at the council offices and Gillian Lye's property. If something sinister turns up, we'll extend the search."

# Chapter Ten

GUS AND BLESSING returned to the cubicle while Phil Crocker set the wheels in motion.

"What can I do to help, guv?" asked Blessing. "You've got several hours of work ahead of you to finish everything by the end of the day."

"I want to speak to the landlord of the Winchester Gate pub, Blessing," said Gus. "DI Stanton will be tied up for hours, especially if they find what I think they'll find. Get hold of whoever's name is now over the door, and ask who was mine host six years ago. I exaggerated slightly about how much time I needed. Chris Stanton isn't going to elbow me out of the way without a fight. We'll continue to make progress until the clock strikes five. Meanwhile, I'll get back to updating the Freeman files. The pub is within easy walking distance, as you can see from the street map behind me. Get over there, find the name of the person we want, and call me. I'll pick you up, and we'll visit them."

"Got it, guv," said Blessing.

She checked the map, realised the Winchester Gate was

less than a quarter of a mile from the police station and set off.

Gus found it tough to concentrate on typing up his notes. But, if he could stop thinking about the telephone engineer and how he connected to Mandy Howard, he would break the back of the task in an hour.

Blessing called him within five minutes.

"Martin Cummings is the landlord," said Blessing. "I've popped outside the pub because the reception isn't great indoors. It's okay. He can't hear me. Mr Cummings is older than you, guv. He's been at the Winchester Gate for seven years. It's quiet here for the next hour, so he reckoned. If you want to talk to him, he said now's perfect. Shall I tell him you're on your way?"

"Give me five minutes, Blessing," said Gus.

When Gus entered the old pub, it reminded him of several hostelries he visited during his time in the city. Blessing was perched on a bar stool while Martin Cummings, the current landlord, stood behind the counter, arms folded across an ample stomach.

"Mr Freeman, I presume," said the white-haired gentleman, who Gus gauged to be in his early seventies. Cummings stuck out a hand the size of a dinner plate, and they shook hands.

"Thank you for agreeing to meet me, Mr Cummings," said Gus. "My colleague tells me Mandy Howard worked for you before her death."

"Call me Martin, please," said the landlord. "I told your young lady that a pub has stood on this corner since the seventeenth century. Although, it only became a free house called the Winchester Gate in 1974. Mandy was one of the first people I took on after I moved here. The name Freeman rings a bell. Have you lived in Salisbury long?"

"I was born here, Martin," said Gus, "and worked here until I retired to a village near Devizes in 2015. How long have you been a publican?"

"Forty years, give or take," said Martin. "I've run half a dozen premises in the city."

"Well, I've drunk in several pubs in the city," laughed Gus. "The fact I don't recognise you must mean you didn't play fast and loose with the terms of your licence, nor did you allow criminals to make your pub their local."

"It could mean I was lucky," said Martin. "When I started, I ran a small place, basically a two-up two-down cottage where the ground-floor rooms were turned into a public bar and a saloon. Our accommodation was upstairs, and we didn't need a kitchen because serving food wasn't essential then."

"You had low prices and simple furnishings in the public bar," said Gus. "The middle-class customers paid a few pence more for their pint and enjoyed a little more comfort in the saloon. The British class system in all its glory for everyone to see."

"Very true. We outgrew that place in a couple of years," said Martin. "I felt confident we could run a bigger pub, and after we moved there, we were among the first to introduce bar snacks."

"Sausage and chips in a basket," said Gus. "The good old days."

"The bad old days now," said Martin. "What were we thinking? We gave everyone a plastic knife and fork. That wouldn't be allowed these days. Are you two staying for a while? Can I get you a drink?"

"We're on duty," said Blessing. "Mr Freeman has to drive back to Devizes later."

"I can get you any coffee you want, miss," said Martin.

"A big percentage of our customers have never tasted alcohol. No wonder pubs are closing every week around us. That's the trouble with teetotallers. I enjoy a drink, and when I wake up with a hangover, I know it will be some time before I feel great again. Teetotallers, when they wake up, that's as good as they will feel all day."

Blessing giggled.

"Dean Martin," said Gus.

"Who?" asked Blessing.

"It doesn't matter, Blessing," said Gus. "Which pub were you running when the ring road came through here?"

"The Conquered Moon on Woodside Road. It opened on July 24th 1969, the year of the first moon landing. We had two bars and a children's room. Unfortunately, the Moon closed in 2004, and now it's been demolished."

"I haven't spent much time in the city since I retired," said Gus. "The past couple of days here have stirred so many memories. Do you remember the house just along the road from here that locals always called number 88?"

"I do. The new road went straight through that spot, didn't it?" said Martin.

"Yeah, it went past the top of Milford Street," said Gus. "You couldn't see that street before because of that old wooden house. It was a pity they needed to knock that down."

"Everyone around here was up in arms when the house and hall were purchased for demolition. They heard it would be re-erected at Lockeridge, near Marlborough, but it never happened," said Martin. "That building had been there since the fifteenth century. All those timber beams and original brick chimney stack. Do you remember the roof? It bore the last surviving mediaeval ridge tile finial in the city —a historic building like that had to go because of the ring road. Forty years on, and plenty want us to walk, ride a bike, and abandon cars altogether. If only we'd known, we could have laid down before the bulldozers and stopped them from destroying our heritage."

Martin prepared three coffees at the other end of the bar and brought them to the counter.

"I've got one person serving here this afternoon. The bar won't get busy until early evening. So, if there's anything you want to ask about Mandy, I'm free."

"Did Mandy come to work for you soon after she moved into Rampart Road?" asked Gus.

"She dropped in with her partner for a drink," said Martin. "I recognised her from before. She saw from a sign in the window that I was looking for someone to do a few hours in the week, plus work every Saturday night. Mandy offered to work three nights in total. Every Saturday, and the other two to fit with whatever I needed. It was great to have the flexibility. She started straightaway, and, well, you know the rest."

"You said you recognised Mandy from before," said Gus. "She hadn't been in Salisbury long."

"Mandy became a regular visitor at the pub I took on after the Conquered Moon closed as soon as she arrived in Salisbury," said Martin. "My wife told me it was a mistake to move there. It had always had the reputation of being a younger person's pub. We were getting too old for the loud music, and with the later opening, we had our share of trouble. My bar staff and the people on the door had to have eyes in the back of their heads. You know what kids are like these days. Mr Freeman. Not just the kids, either. It was impossible to control everything. Perhaps it was wrong, but I told the staff to ignore it if they spotted a bit of cannabis use, but I drew the line at hard drugs. Mandy and her partner liked a smoke, but I guess you knew that."

"We did," said Gus. "Was John Crees also a regular at this music venue of yours?"

"I think I would have noticed him if he was, don't you?" said Martin.

Gus remembered something Emily Farrell had told him.

"Did you have live music every week?"

"Every Friday and Saturday," said Martin. "It was expected. Even though we couldn't persuade the punters to pay for the privilege, the only way we could compete with the other pubs in the city was to stump up the fees for a local band and hope we got enough in takings by staying open after midnight. Several others close at midnight as we do here, and we only needed two dozen youngsters, already well on the way to being drunk, to pile in to listen to the bands and keep drinking."

"What time did you set as the deadline for entry?" asked Gus.

"Half-past eleven," said Martin. "The locals soon worked out they could listen to the band's second set and get their first round of drinks at normal prices. We added ten pence to everything after midnight to help defray our extra overheads."

"You were forced to have door staff because of the late licence," said Gus. "Was it still profitable?"

"Probably not, but it's a trade-off. When you've got people in your pub for a couple of hours on a weekend night, you need to make sure they see lots of signage offering good deals in the week. Two steak meals for a tenner on Tuesday, a free pool table on Thursday; anything to keep them coming back."

"We believe John Crees met Mandy at your previous

pub on a Bank Holiday weekend," said Gus. "One of her colleagues told us you had live music on four consecutive nights. Do you remember that occasion?"

"Hard to forget," said Martin. "The opportunity for a bumper weekend doesn't come around too often. So we pushed the boat out and booked the most popular covers bands in the region. Mandy was there every night, and the place was crowded. My wife persuaded me to erect a bouncy castle in the car park and add straw bales, extra tables, and umbrellas. The weather was perfect for a change, and families came during the day; our kitchen staff were run off their feet, and although the bands didn't start playing until later in the evening, I gave punters free access to the jukebox. So we had wall-to-wall music from eleven in the morning."

"I can imagine that didn't go down too well with the neighbours," said Blessing.

"We had the correct licences," shrugged Martin. "But the killjoys were on the warpath in September. We knew we wouldn't get the chance to run an event like that again. We might have got away with it if we hadn't had the trouble on Monday night."

"Too many hot summer days and nights drinking," said Gus. "Fights broke out as the event drew to a close, I suppose?"

"One of our most popular bands caused the crowd to get feisty," said Martin. "They'd played their first set from eight until nine. We had four bands; the others were paid for a one-hour set. At midnight, I expected the first band to return to play for forty-five minutes. I'd told their singer they could do a couple of encores, but they should not be playing after one o'clock. I wasn't watching what was happening on the makeshift stage in the main bar, but the singer came across and called me over. He said their guitarist had walked out on them, and without their star performer, they couldn't go on."

"What was the reason for the guitarist walking out?" asked Gus. "An argument with other band members? Perhaps he was unhappy with the money they were getting paid. The other groups only had to play for an hour, and they had to hang around for three hours before doing a late shift."

"We paid the going rate for each of the bands we used. Nobody had cause for complaint on that score," said Martin. "That particular group had performed for us many times without any problems. I did ask the singer whether there had been a difference of opinion. He didn't know of anything. I wondered whether the row had been with one of the other groups or if someone in the crowd had said something to annoy the bloke. Nobody seemed to know why he left."

"What happened next?" asked Gus.

"I told the singer to explain to the crowd why they wouldn't be playing," said Martin. "I wanted everyone to know it wasn't my fault. The jukebox was turned back on as soon as he'd delivered the bad news. It went down like a lead balloon, as you can imagine. Scuffles broke out in the bar, and our staff got the troublemakers outside into the car park. That was when the fights escalated."

"You regretted covering the car park with extra tables, straw bales, and umbrellas," said Gus. "The door staff now had a small crowd of drunken youngsters with room to move and ammunition."

"I soon heard the ruckus outside and called the police," said Martin. "If the killjoys didn't have enough to stop us from holding another event like that before, they did then.

That was the beginning of the end at that pub for the wife and me. After that, we started looking for a smaller place with character where we could have a quiet path to retirement. We didn't need the hassle."

"So, you didn't see John Crees that weekend?" asked Gus.

"I said he wasn't a regular," said Martin. "When Mandy came to work here, she did mention they had met in my old pub. It could have been that Bank Holiday weekend. As I said, the place was crowded all four nights, and Mandy was one of our proper regulars. She made a point of coming to speak to me at the bar like she always did. You need to step back and take a five-minute breather on a long day like that. More often when you're my age, so, when there was a lull, I'd let the younger ones cope with the drinks orders and come to the other side of the bar for a break. If she spotted me at times like that, Mandy would always come over for a chat. She'd tell me how much she was enjoying the music or ask whether the band had ever heard the original version of the track they were murdering. The usual small talk, you know. We talked about the weather, I asked how work was going, and she said she was happy enough. Mandy and I had conversations like that all the time. We carried on in the same vein while she worked here. Mandy was a good person, Mr Freeman."

"Someone didn't think so, Martin," said Gus. "I see you have live music here, despite the problems it caused before."

"Only on a Saturday night," said Martin. "Because of where we're situated, most of our regulars can walk here. We're on their doorstep, being on Rampart Street, and we don't want to fall out with our neighbours. So, we close at midnight, and the music stops by a quarter to twelve."

"Do you use the same bands you booked at the old venue?" asked Blessing.

"Some of them have been around for a decade or more," said Martin. "They're popular with the punters, and we'd suffer a loss of revenue if we kicked them into the long grass. Band members come and go, so we can see familiar faces suddenly turning up in a different line-up."

"What about the group that let you down on that Bank Holiday Monday?" asked Gus.

"They must have split up," said Martin. "I've forgotten their name for the minute, but I have had the singer in here with his new band. They call themselves Down South, but the set list hasn't altered much from what he did before. The guitarist isn't a patch on the guy who walked out that night; he was mustard. They were one of the bands that had been around for years. The singer must be in his early fifties, and the other band members were in the same age bracket. The guitarist looked the part, you know, tall, with long hair, despite his age, and he hadn't put on the pounds in middle age like some of us, either. I'd be surprised if he didn't play professionally in his youth. He reminded me of Jeff Beck to look at, and almost as good."

"What did Mandy think of the band he played with?" asked Gus.

"They were one of her favourites," said Martin. "She wasn't a groupie. Please don't think that of her. Mandy was friendly with several blokes who drank in the pub, and sometimes she'd chat to a band member, but it never went anywhere. I never got the impression she was looking for a long-term relationship when she first moved here."

"Did Mandy ever speak about relationships she'd had back in Wales?" asked Blessing.

"The police asked me that question after the murder,"

said Martin. "Just before they dropped the case due to lack of progress, I suppose. Then, one night when we were quiet and the band was taking a break, Mandy told me that she'd been seeing someone in Merthyr for a couple of years, and it didn't end well. I was surprised the police didn't follow that up."

"Interesting, guv," said Blessing.

"Perhaps," said Gus. "Were all the bands you booked semi-professional? Or did any of them do it full-time?"

"As far as I know, they had other jobs," said Martin. "It's not any of my business, is it? Still, Al Capone was arrested for tax evasion, so I should keep quiet. I never ask whether their tax affairs are in order, Mr Freeman. I'm sorry."

"Don't worry," said Gus. "That wasn't what was on my mind. The clouds will pass in time, and I'll see things clearly."

"Clouds," said Martin Cummings. "That's it. I've remembered the name of that band now. When that guitarist played with them, they called themselves Nimbus."

Gus finished his coffee, thanked Martin Cummings for his time, and returned to Bourne Hill with Blessing.

"Was that useful, guv?" she asked.

"Yet again, most of it ties in with what we already knew," said Gus. "Phil Crocker had various leads he wanted to follow after the raid on the bikers' clubhouse, but his superiors closed the book once the intimidation started. According to what she said in her interview with Crocker and Mears, Mandy never mentioned a failed relationship to Gillian Lye. There was nothing to suggest Mandy feared an ex-boyfriend was about to ride, or drive, across the Severn Bridge to drag her back to South Wales."

When they reached the cubicle, Gus grabbed the laptop

and started typing from his notebook. Blessing was at a loose end.

"Can I do something useful, guv?" she asked. "We've still got forty-five minutes before we leave."

"Phone the Winchester Gate, Blessing," said Gus. "I meant to ask Martin Cummings for the name of that singer and the guitarist if he knows it. He'll have a business card for the group in his office."

"Leave it with me, guv," said Blessing. "So I don't disturb you, I'll use the empty cubicle next door. Then, I'll start packing our things, ready to transfer to the office."

Gus nodded and carried on typing.

He didn't have as much time to himself as he wanted. The next time he looked up, Phil Crocker stood before him.

"The forensic people couldn't find anything odd about Emily Farrell's phone, sorry," said Phil. "We thanked her for the message she sent you, though. Are you nearly finished?"

"Forty-five minutes, sir," said Gus.

"Good. Hang on, that's my phone."

Gus made a mental to call Emily Farrell.

Phil hurried back from his office.

"Noah Baker has just heard from the forensic people at Hilltop Way," said Phil. "They found a bug in Gillian's home phone. Noah's getting permission to access her bank accounts. We need to discover whether she had a telecoms engineer visit her while Mandy was living there or soon after. Sadly, we haven't got Gillian's mobile, so we can't check whether that was bugged too."

"I think the fact the killer took it with him means that's a given, sir," said Gus. "If he'd ripped the home phone from the wall, it would have looked suspicious. He took a chance we wouldn't think Gillian was being closely monitored.

Blessing had finished her phone call to Martin Cummings and returned to the cubicle.

"Good afternoon, sir," she said.

"It's one-all on the phone bugs, DC Umeh," said Phil Crocker. "Emily Farrell was clean, and as your boss suspected, we found one in the house at Hilltop Way."

"That makes sense, sir," said Emily. "If that engineer had targeted a phone in the Housing Department office, it would have been the one on Mandy's desk."

"Emily told me she kept remembering how Mandy was when she sat at the desk behind me," said Gus. "So, the desk may still be there. I don't recall seeing a phone on it, though. Can you go and check, please?"

"On it, guv," said Blessing. "His name was Paul Price, by the way, guv,"

"Who, the telecoms engineer?" asked Phil Crocker.

"No, um, it doesn't matter, sir. Forget I spoke."

Blessing hurried away before she dropped them both in it.

"She's still learning, sir," said Gus. "I have to make allowances."

"Are you sure you didn't leave the office for a while, Gus?"

"We needed to walk off the effects of the large pasty we had for lunch, sir," said Gus.

"A likely tale," said Phil. "Remember what I said. Please leave it to Chris Stanton and Noah Baker.

Phil Crocker disappeared to answer another phone call. Gus finished typing and read through the information they'd collected since Kenneth Truelove had handed him the murder file.

Five minutes later, Blessing was back from the Housing

Department office, and Gus was checking the first pages of the hard copy he'd printed for DI Stanton.

"Paul Price, Blessing," said Gus. "Did you get those contact details?"

"Yes, guv," said Blessing. "I nearly put my foot in it, didn't I?"

"I think Phil Crocker knew we wouldn't stop sticking our nose in," said Gus. "Anything else?"

"I asked Emily Farrell how old she thought the engineer was," said Blessing. "Emily said he had to be fifty, but his long hair was still dark. When I asked about the desks, Emily said they'd all been changed three years ago, and a newer model replaced the old phone system. The council employed a different firm to instal that. So, anything we might have found will have gone in a skip long ago."

"That means Mandy could have had a bug in her office phone in 2012," said Gus. "Right, I've almost finished printing the stuff DI Stanton said he wanted. Finish clearing everything we want to take, and lock it in my car. Take my keys."

Gus handed several sheets of paper and his car keys to Blessing.

"What are you going to do, guv?" she asked.

"I'll pop across the office to say cheerio to Bob Mears," said Gus. "Then I'd better do the same to DCI Crocker. I'll see you in the car park in ten minutes."

Blessing started opening drawers and piling their bits and pieces on the desk.

Bob looked over a pile of files when he sensed someone was nearby.

"Are you ready for the off then, Gus?" asked Bob.

"Nearly there, Bob," said Gus. "We popped into the

Winchester Gate for an hour earlier and spoke to the landlord, Martin Cummings."

"I remember him," said Bob. "Didn't give us a lot. Mandy started working for him at the pub soon after she moved in with Spider Crees. She was a good worker, never let him down, and he was able to confirm the details about the last night she worked there. Why?"

"Did you check any pubs he'd run before the Winchester Gate?" asked Gus.

"Why should we? Cummings was never a suspect. We followed leads thrown up from the interviews we had with her work colleagues and landlady," said Bob. "We were focussing on the Hells Angel connection. Nobody had a bad word to say about Mandy, and nobody's name was put in the frame as someone she argued with."

"Martin Cummings ran the pub where Mandy met Spider Crees," said Gus. "She was a regular, a fact confirmed by Gillian Lye. He told us this afternoon that Mandy always chatted to him whenever she was in the pub."

"So they knew one another before she moved to Rampart Road," said Bob. "Then she walked two hundred yards from her house and replied to an ad in the pub window for bar staff. So what? We spoke to people who used that music venue, and nobody gave us a name worthy of a closer look."

"Perhaps they were looking in the wrong direction," said Gus.

"Did Cummings give you anything else to make you think we messed up?" asked Bob.

"Because nobody asked Martin Cummings the right questions, you didn't learn that in those conversations with Martin, Mandy let on she'd been in a relationship in

Merthyr. Two years it had lasted before an acrimonious break-up. I don't know how long before she moved to Salisbury, but it might have been worth finding out, don't you think?"

"We checked for strangers in Salisbury, Gus," said Bob. "Phil checked the Severn Bridge cameras and the trains. Unfortunately, we couldn't trace anyone matching the timeline."

"I don't think it was a jilted lover, Bob," said Gus. "If Mandy had been afraid someone might knock on the door one night, she would have told Gillian Lye after a few glasses of wine. No, the answer lies elsewhere, and DI Stanton has a vague description of a suspect who installed a bug in Gillian Lye's home phone."

"Blimey. You were right, " said Bob. "I miss working on that type of case. I'm resigned to being a glorified file clerk until they retire me."

"What will you do when you're free of this place, Bob?" asked Gus.

"I won't be playing golf, that's for sure," scoffed Bob. "I've got my lurchers to exercise, and they'll keep me fit and out from under the wife's feet."

"I'll let you get back to your files," said Gus. "I could see more of your head as I crossed the office. So you're making progress."

"Don't make me laugh," said Bob. "If you spotted it, so will Phil, and he'll find another batch to add to my misery."

Gus left Bob Mears to wallow in self-pity and returned to the cubicle to fetch the final hard copies. He checked everything was in the correct order and went to say goodbye to Phil Crocker.

"Here we are, sir, all present and correct."

"Thanks, Gus," said Phil. "Once again, I'm sorry things

turned out this way, but nobody anticipated Gillian Lye's murder."

"It can't be helped, sir," said Gus. "We'll get back to the Old Police Station office in the morning, and Geoff Mercer will probably be on the phone at five past nine with new orders."

Phil Crocker got up, came around his large desk, and shook Gus by the hand.

"Good luck with everything, Gus. The baby and any future cases the Chief Constable hands you."

"Thank you, sir," said Gus. He left the office, went downstairs, and joined Blessing outside.

"All set, guv?" she asked.

"Do we have everything, Blessing?" asked Gus.

"Yes, guv," she replied. "So does DI Stanton now. Do you think he'll solve the case?"

Gus smiled.

"I would like to think so, Blessing. DCI Crocker asked me at lunchtime to hand over everything we'd collected since we arrived. That's what we've done. He forgot to specify that anything we learned later this afternoon should be included."

# Chapter Eleven

"THAT'S why you gave me those few sheets of paper," said Blessing. "I did wonder. You rescued them from the printer. That was sneaky."

"What is it they say, Blessing? It's not my first rodeo? I took the precaution of sowing a few seeds in Bob Mears's ear before I left the office. He'll make sure his old boss hears about the ex-boyfriend from the Welsh Valleys, and, with luck, Stanton and Baker will be out of our hair for a few days. I don't expect them to leave until they see the autopsy results on Thursday. They wouldn't want to jump the gun. Meanwhile, Bob insisted he and Phil had spoken to enough pubgoers from Martin Cummings's music venue to gauge whether anyone had a grudge against Mandy Howard. So, when he whispers in Phil Crocker's ear that they missed her friend, Martin Cummings, it will provide another delaying tactic for Phil's blue-eyed boys."

"Can I tell Grace what's happened today when I see her tonight, guv?" asked Blessing.

"Do you think it wise?" asked Gus.

"Silence is golden, guv," said Blessing. "Am I right?"

"Exactly," said Gus. "I think it's high time you moved up the ladder, DC Umeh. As you know, it's a four-step process to become a sergeant. You've proved to be a quick learner, and I'm confident you've achieved competence in your current post. That's step one. Next, you must study hard for the exam on law and procedure, then thirdly, you should be on the lookout for local vacancies that match your aspirations. DS Mercer and I will do our utmost to see you settled as soon as possible. A work-based assessment will follow one year after your temporary promotion, and Bob's your uncle."

"I'm not sure I want to work with Bob Mears, guv," said Blessing.

"That's not quite what I meant, but never mind," said Gus. "Let's get you back to Worton."

Forty minutes later, Gus had dropped her off at the farm and headed toward Urchfont.

Suzie must have arrived home just before him. She had parked her Golf and collected things from the back seat as Gus swung the Focus through the gateway.

"Let's get inside, away from the cold wind," she said when Gus joined her at the side of the bungalow. "I didn't expect to see you carrying that large folder again. Didn't you get the lockable filing cabinet you were after?"

Gus went through the day's events in the kitchen as they prepared a meal. He glossed over the postscript to the Freeman files that had somehow gone astray. The fewer people that knew about that, the better.

"It seems fairly straightforward to me," said Suzie as they sat in the lounge with a cup of coffee after they'd eaten.

"I'd appreciate hearing what you believe happened,"

said Gus. "I can get too close to a case in its early stages and not see a flaw in my reasoning. I hope you don't assume the worst, but I've found giving the case my full attention difficult. Every corner I turn in Salisbury evokes a long-forgotten memory. That never happened when I lived and worked there."

"You didn't have long-forgotten memories for a lot of the time then, darling," said Suzie. "When I was still driving to the farm on a Saturday morning to tend to my horse, I'd be brushing her down, and I'd recall a Pony Club competition I'd won with her. It's only natural. You walked the city streets for decades, so there's a potential memory around every corner. I don't think it's a sign you're getting senile."

"I'm wondering why it's happening now, " Gus said. "Does one of those memories connect to the murder case we've been reviewing, or is it because I'll be out on my ear once Kenneth and Geoff have retired? Déjà vu all over again."

"I can't see how anything in your past can connect with the case from what you've told me this evening," said Suzie. "That niggle you had hasn't been resolved, though. So let me give you my thoughts, and perhaps that will trigger something."

"Fire away," said Gus.

"Mandy Howard left Merthyr after a relationship ended," said Suzie. "When she arrived in Salisbury, she lived with Gillian Lye. Mandy was happy in her work life and had a social life that didn't include her work colleagues or landlady. Mandy enjoyed visiting pubs with live music and rode her bike at weekends. How's that so far?"

"Nothing to argue with yet," said Gus.

"Mandy had lived and worked in the city for a year when she met John Crees at her favourite music venue. It was a long Bank Holiday weekend with great weather. We don't know which night they met, but they continued seeing one another and started living together in a house on Rampart Road in the autumn of 2010. They spent their weekends riding their bikes and smoking weed."

"That's your first slip-up," said Gus. "We do know exactly which night they met."

Suzie thought for a moment.

"Monday night," she said. "My mistake. The guitarist didn't have a tantrum until Monday at midnight. So, based on Emily Farrell's description of the telecoms engineer, you believe the guitarist was the creepy-looking guy Emily remembered messing with their phones when the council people were moving into offices at Bourne Hill."

"Emily told me she saw how the engineer kept glancing at Mandy and sensed her colleague disliked him," said Gus. "She didn't ask Mandy why that was or where she knew him from then. They were too busy with the move. There could be two tall, dark men, in their fifties, with long hair in Salisbury, but Mandy's reaction makes me think they were one and the same. Blessing got contact details for the band from the landlord of the Winchester Gate this afternoon."

"So, did you pass those details to the detectives in the case?" asked Suzie.

"They could be well out of date after six years," said Gus. "Carry on with your thought processes, darling."

"You won't get off the hook that easy, Gus Freeman," said Suzie. "Right, fast-forward to Friday afternoon, and you phone Gillian Lye and catch her just before she leaves her desk in the Adult Care Department. Gillian tells you she's got a busy three days ahead but doesn't elaborate and agrees to meet you at her house on Hilltop Way tomorrow morning at ten. After she returned from her conference weekend near Swindon, she was strangled in her front room. The killer takes her mobile phone, but nothing else from inside the house besides her car keys. They then drive to the far side of the Country Park and set the car alight. Did the forensic people find charred remains of a mobile phone inside?"

"I'm no longer on the case, so I'm not privy to that information," said Gus.

"You believed, as soon as you heard about the suspicious death at Hilltop Way, that the killer had to have been listening in on your conversation," said Suzie.

"It was the only thing that made sense," said Gus. "Gillian was still at work, and a colleague might have overheard her speaking to me. Also, Gillian wasn't in the best of health; her death could have been due to natural causes. However, once Bob Martin told me Daisy Field had received a call from Gillian on Sunday evening, extending her holiday by an extra half-day, it was clear the covert surveillance extended to Gillian's mobile phone. That phone call had sealed her fate. The killer made their way to Hilltop Way, arriving just before Gillian reached home. The attack came within seconds of the poor woman getting through the front door, and a third murder was then committed. The killer tried to cover their tracks, but not as skilfully as they had back in 2012."

"They should have set fire to part of the property," said Suzie. "Throw in a few random extras, and they could have destroyed the house phone and the mobile. The discovery of the bug by the forensic team has given DI Stanton a solid lead. Something Phil Crocker and Bob Mears didn't have six years ago."

"I'm not so sure about that," said Gus.

"What, that DI Stanton has a solid lead?" asked Suzie.

"No, I think Crocker and Mears might have heard something six years ago but didn't give it a second thought. I wouldn't have pursued the slender thread if it wasn't for the building development."

"You've lost me," said Suzie.

"I won't know whether I'm right until we track down that guitarist," said Gus. "I'm convinced he's responsible for all three murders, but the motive for one is unclear."

"You do remember you've been side-lined, don't you?" asked Suzie. "What did Geoff Mercer tell you to do?"

"I haven't spoken to him yet," said Gus. "Phil Crocker mentioned Farm Watch to Blessing in passing, but even that was only a possibility. Nothing was cast in stone. Blessing and I will drive to the Old Police Station office in the morning. Phil Crocker said we were to await further instructions."

"Your earlier comments suggest you plan to continue working on the case," said Suzie. "Please think twice before you put yourself and Blessing in danger."

"We have to do something while we wait for Geoff to find time in his busy day," said Gus. "What could be dangerous about the odd phone call from the safety of our first-floor office anyway?"

"Sarah Holland and her colleagues will be there tomorrow, don't forget," said Suzie. "I'd check your phones if I were you. What if a telecoms engineer went to your office to instal their equipment and messed with yours too?"

"We'd be bugged," said Gus. "Or something with another two letters."

"You're incorrigible," said Suzie.

"Don't worry, I'll be careful," said Gus. "It might be tricky to squeeze a few interviews in between whatever Geoff has in store for us, but I took precautions. If things work out, Stanton and Baker shouldn't be snapping at my heels until early next week."

"You plan to have the case done and dusted by then, I presume?"

"I don't want Sylvia Robbins to start work in January and find us dithering over the original cold case review," said Gus. "I'd like to have the whole team back with a new case from Kenneth's top drawer. I refuse to go out with a defeat against the CRT's name. Even worse, I don't want her arriving at London Road and hearing that two youngsters from Bourne Hill cracked a case that I couldn't, despite having all the pieces of the jigsaw. No way am I standing aside for Stanton and Baker to take the credit for merely picking up the new information Blessing and I uncovered and then joining the dots."

"Have you thought what Phil Crocker might do if he finds out you're disobeying orders?" asked Suzie. "He could make things very unpleasant for the Crime Review Team. You already suspect Sylvia Robbins will be looking for the flimsiest excuse to fire you. Why hand her the bullets?"

"What's life without a little risk?" asked Gus. He looked at the clock. "Time for bed."

"As I said, incorrigible," sighed Suzie.

## Tuesday, 4 December 2018

GUS AND SUZIE were back in the old routine, if only for a day. Suzie awoke at seven-fifteen and went to the bathroom. Gus went to the kitchen ten minutes later and started breakfast. When Suzie emerged from the bathroom after her shower, Gus took her place while Suzie took over in the kitchen.

They sat together just before eight with a nourishing bowl of vegetable soup.

"Coffee after soup always feels wrong," said Suzie as Gus poured himself a cup

"The start of a day without coffee would be ten times wrong," said Gus. "I slept well, considering. Your analysis of the case didn't throw up any howlers. Unfortunately, the details are a tad ruffled at present. I need to iron out a few creases."

Suzie loaded the dishwasher while Gus got his things together. The murder file and several separate sheets were lying on the coffee table in the lounge where they'd left them.

"Coats and scarves again today, darling," said Suzie as they stepped outside.

"I hope Sarah and her colleagues haven't played with the thermostat in the office," said Gus. "I can't think clearly when my fingers and toes have frostbite."

Suzie tutted and led the way to the cars.

The sleety rain had eased, but the north wind was still doing its worst.

"Drive safely, sweetheart," said Gus.

He followed her Golf into Devizes and acknowledged Suzie's wave as she peeled off for London Road. Gus parked the Focus at the far left end of the CRT's designated parking bays twenty minutes later. Geoff Mercer hadn't increased the quota yet, to allow for the newcomers. Blessing reversed into a bay at the other end of the row as Gus waited for the lift.

"Good morning, guv," she said. "Have you noticed?"

"They nicked our parking bays without a by-your-leave," said Gus.

"Well, that too, guv," said Blessing. "I spotted that all three cars were registered in September."

"It makes sense, " said Gus as the lift doors opened. "After buying this lot new cars, they couldn't afford a separate office. So they were forced to slum it with us."

Blessing was still giggling when they emerged into the first-floor office.

"Good morning, Freeman," said Stuart Midwinter.

Gus hadn't noticed the PCC's car in the car park.

"Good morning, sir," said Gus.

"Who we have here?" asked the PCC, looking at Blessing.

"DC Umeh, sir," said Blessing. "I was transferred from the Farm Watch initiative to work with Mr Freeman at Bourne Hill Police Station."

"Of course," said Midwinter. "A somewhat unusual set of events, would you agree?"

"Someone I phoned last Friday died on Sunday night, sir," said Gus. "I don't consider that unusual. It was a logical consequence of the intercepted phone call. The killer had bugged people's phones directly connected to Mandy Howard. The killer was convinced that their secret would be revealed if I asked the right questions of the right people."

"Quite," said Midwinter. "Well, you don't need to worry about that now. DCI Crocker has a first-class detective team on the case. Whether the latest murder is connected to your cold case remains to be seen, but for you to keep treading on his team's toes is untenable. DC Mercer will give you something to tide you over until the holidays. Then, all things being equal, you'll be here with almost a full complement in early January."

Gus wanted to ask what 'almost' meant, but Stuart Midwinter was in full flow. He introduced the members of his team. Gus and Blessing nodded and smiled in all the right places.

Morris Beard, the Strategic Delivery Lead for Prevention and Youth, seemed keen to justify the department's existence. Gus thought he looked on the right side of fifty, while he already knew that Sarah Holland and Rosie Allison were close to Suzie's age. The same as Grace if it came to that.

"I know moving in yesterday must have been hectic," said Gus. "Was there anything you wanted to ask?"

"We came in on Sunday," said Morris. "We're all set, thanks. It would have badly impacted our timetable if we'd left everything until yesterday. We have a voluntary, confidential, early intervention programme underway that supports people at risk of being drawn into crime. If support isn't deemed appropriate, they may be signposted to other safeguarding services for help. That support includes help with mental health, drug, or alcohol abuse issues, education, and career advice."

"I was given the bare bones of what you're responsible for when the Chief Constable told me you were moving here," said Gus. "Two of my Detective Sergeants have been assigned to Gablecross, temporarily, to assist with your early-intervention scheme. Whether they've found anyone prepared to listen to what they have to offer, I don't know. I'm hoping to get feedback from them on Friday."

"Taking part in the voluntary scheme doesn't go on someone's criminal record and won't negatively impact their future education or career prospects," said Rosie Allison. "It means getting the right kind of help for the person who needs support to avoid getting drawn into criminal activities. Working with hard-to-reach groups, improving chances of not becoming a victim of exploitation and preventing crime from happening is as much of a key issue for policing as answering 999 calls."

Blessing wished she could escape to the restroom. Gus would need a black coffee soon, and her head was spinning.

"We've got a TV crew here in fifteen minutes, Mr Freeman," said Morris Beard. "We don't make a habit of it, but Stuart thought the scheme would benefit from the publicity. It gives us a chance to show the public where we work and that we're committed to improving the lives of young people."

"Terrific," said Gus. "We won't be in the way, will we?"

"Have you heard from DS Mercer yet?" asked Midwinter.

"Not yet, sir," said Gus.

"If you could show the crew up when they ring the bell, Freeman, and lay low. There's a good chap. It might be best to turn your phones off while they're here."

Gus and Blessing exchanged glances. She headed for the restroom.

Three faces soon appeared on the camera showing the area outside the lift. Gus recognised the BBC Points West reporter, buzzed the crew in, and pointed towards the far end of the room when they emerged into the office. Then he resumed drinking the cup of black coffee Blessing had brought him.

"I'm going to call DS Mercer from the restroom," said Gus. Blessing sat and watched the pantomime ahead of her as lights were set up around a desk, and a microphone was secured to the PCC's suit jacket. Gus hadn't returned, but

Blessing could hear the introductions had been made, and the PCC was about to do his piece to the camera.

"A specialist Youth and Early Intervention team, which consists of police officers, PCSOs, police staff and an analyst, means there is a one-team approach and ensures continuity and collaboration for our communities. This early intervention model seeks to identify and address the root causes of issues for children and families at the earliest opportunity before they become entrenched in exploitative or criminal activities. Strong evidence supports that effective early intervention can significantly improve the lives of young people, diverting them from anti-social behaviour and criminal activity."

Gus opened the restroom door, and try as he might, he couldn't cross the room to his desk without kicking a chair.

"Cut," said the reporter. "We'll try that again."

"Let's go, Blessing," said Gus.

When they were safely in the lift, Blessing asked:

"Was that an accident, guv?"

"I couldn't hang about in the restroom until the PCC had finished. We're off to Salisbury."

"What did DS Mercer say, guv?" asked Blessing.

"Vera Butler told me he was in a meeting until lunchtime. So, we can track down Paul Price without interference."

"The business card I got from Martin Cummings is a bit dog-eared, guv," said Blessing. "His address when this was printed was in a village called Sparsholt. I've found it on the map, and it's a couple of miles west of Winchester."

"We'll start there, and if he's moved, with luck, the new people will have a forwarding address."

Gus drove them towards Salisbury and then turned towards Andover.

"There's a turn-off for the Amesbury bypass, guv," said Blessing. "I've been that way before with Neil while investigating the librarian's murder."

"We don't need to go into Salisbury to get to the village you mentioned," said Gus. "What was the exact address?"

"Wood Lane, guv," said Blessing.

A little over an hour after leaving the Old Police Station office, Gus drew up outside The Plough public house in Sparsholt.

"Mr Price lives in one of the houses further along the lane, guv," said Blessing.

"Perhaps," said Gus, "but the village pub is always a good place to call for information. Plus, I didn't use the facilities before I left the restroom. Wait here. I'll be back."

Gus ducked his head as he went inside. Blessing looked around the car park. The pub had just opened, and there were just two other cars. So Gus wouldn't have many customers to quiz for information on Paul Price.

Five minutes later, Gus was back.

"Right, Paul Price lives in the cottage next door. He's working today, and his wife is a lecturer at the College and University Centre on Westley Lane. Not a bad setup. His wife can walk to work in just over a quarter of an hour, and the couple have a pub on their doorstep."

"You've got a pub just along the lane, guv," said Blessing. "It seems an odd place for a college, though. What can you study there?"

"Rural studies," said Gus. "Courses on agriculture, forestry, animal and zoo management. I didn't ask whether Mrs Price was the nation's leading export on hippopotamuses because we're only interested in the husband. I learned that Paul Price is working at the Calvert Centre."

"Does his band have a gig there, guv?" asked Blessing. "Early for that, isn't it?

"No, it's an industrial estate, Blessing. The landlord said we'd recognise the singer's truck. The business name on the side of the trailer is a giveaway. He's called it The Right Price."

"What business is he in then, guv?" asked Blessing.

"Patience is a virtue, Blessing," said Gus. "We'll be there soon. The landlord told me we needed to hurry; Mr Price is due at another industrial estate in an hour."

Blessing sat quietly as Gus eased the Focus into traffic on the M3. Then, after a rare short burst of speed from her boss, they turned into the industrial estate. She spotted the bright sign on the trailer at once, but there was no sign of Paul Price.

"There he is," said Gus, pointing towards the grassy bank at the side of the estate. A man wearing a yellow hard-hat, hi-viz waistcoat, and ear defenders was trimming the grass verge on a ride-on mini-mower.

Blessing and Gus got out of the car and walked towards him.

The mower slowed to a stop, and the man removed the ear defenders.

"Can I help you?"

"Paul Price?" asked Gus.

"That's me," came the reply.

"We're from Wiltshire Police, sir," said Blessing. "I'm DC Umeh. My boss, Mr Freeman, wishes to speak to you about something which happened six or seven years ago. Do you remember Martin Cummings?"

"He's the landlord at the Winchester Gate," said Paul Price. "I've known Martin for years. Six years ago, did you say? Martin wasn't at the Gate then; he had a bigger place on the outskirts of Salisbury."

"A popular music venue," said Blessing. "We know you often played there with your band. What can you tell us about an incident during an August Bank Holiday weekend?"

"I don't remember anything we did to concern the police," said Paul. "We weren't caught up in the fighting that broke out after midnight on Monday. Our kit was safely locked away in our cars. Why, what are you getting at?"

"The fights broke out because your group was unable to fulfil its contract," said Gus. "A guitarist walked out on you. Surely, you remember that?"

"We weren't likely to forget," said Paul. "Ash separated us from the run-of-the-mill cover bands Martin booked that weekend. Then, he stormed off and never played with us again."

"What was his full name?" asked Blessing. "Was Ash short for Ashley? Or was Ash his surname? Where did he live?"

"I can't help you there, I'm afraid," said Paul. "We'd played a gig in Andover one night, and Ash was hanging around at the side of the stage during the set. He came to speak to me afterwards and asked if we needed a guitarist. I told him we were happy being a four-piece. The other guys were listening while breaking the kit down, and nobody was keen on splitting the money five ways. He asked when we were getting together again to practice and if he could turn up. Ash said he'd appreciate the chance to sit in with us for a while, as he was keen to return to the business again."

"Had he played professionally?" asked Gus.

"We could tell Ash was good enough to have done so

when he turned up at our next practice night," said Paul. "But he never went into detail about who he'd played with. He had his guitar and amp and chose a Wishbone Ash track to show what he could do. His guitar work was incredible, and he could sing a bit too. After that night, the nickname Ash stuck, we became a five-piece, and nobody lost out on the money stakes because we were soon commanding a higher fee and securing bookings at better venues. It was a win-win."

"Have you always run your own business?" asked Gus, nodding towards the mower.

"We've never had enough gigs to go full-time," said Paul. "I was lucky enough to get the franchise for the outfit that owns a string of industrial estates in and around Winchester. I choose when I work and in which order I visit the sites. As long as the grass verges are kept tidy, the trees and bushes don't run wild, and I gather up the rubbish, everyone's happy. My previous franchise was for Little Chef, but that went under, which was a pain. After I'd finished work at one of their restaurants, I could pop in for a bite to eat."

"What about Ash?" asked Gus. "What did he do for a living? Where did he live, anyway?"

Paul Price shrugged,

"Blowed if I know. Ash was a private person. The rest of us live in Winchester or nearby and had known one another for years before Ash came on the scene. Once he started gigging with us, things were going well. We told him where the next gig was, and he pitched up in his Vauxhall Combo. I never thought we needed to do a background check. You still haven't told me what this is all about."

"We're trying to trace him," said Gus. "Which is difficult if the band members he spent two or three nights a week with can't tell us where to look. How long was he with you?"

"Two and half years, maybe," said Paul.

"Did he ever let you down?" asked Blessing.

"Never," said Paul.

"You first met him in Andover," said Gus. "Would that be a good place to start?"

"It might have been where he lived," said Paul. "Accents can be misleading, can't they?"

"What do you mean?" asked Blessing.

"Well, you're from the Midlands, aren't you? It's distinctive; you can't muddle it up with somewhere else. Because Ash was a musician, maybe professional in his younger days, he sounded like he came from the London area, with a touch of California thrown in."

"So, a fifty-something guitarist with a mid-Atlantic drawl," said Gus. "You never heard him mention telecoms at all, I suppose?"

"Not as such," said Paul. "But he was a dab hand at fixing any problems with our amps, the PA system, and all manner of electrical problems. I can't tell you whether that was just what he'd picked up on the road or it had been a profession he'd followed in the past."

"The Vauxhall Combo," said Gus. "New or old?"

"The last time I saw Ash, it would have been five years old," said Paul. "As I said, he walked out that night, and although he knew we were due to play at a gig in Winchester on Friday, he never showed. When he quit, he hadn't even asked me for his share of the fees from the Bank Holiday weekend."

"Martin Cummings told us you couldn't explain why he

walked out," said Gus. "Come on; it's been six years. So what does it matter now? Was it a woman?"

"Isn't it always?" said Paul. "Ash had a thing for one of the women who watched us whenever we played in Salisbury. She followed us from venue to venue for at least six months, maybe longer."

"Did you know her?" asked Blessing.

"I'm married," said Paul. "My wife comes to the occasional gig. I make a point of *not* knowing the first names of female fans of our music. I don't want to encourage them to wander over for a chat when my wife's there. Ash was a single bloke, as far as we could tell. He got a lot of attention because of his guitar playing from men and women, and I guess he was easy on the eye."

"What does that mean?" asked Blessing.

"Look at me," said Paul. "I'm balding, late-fifties, and built like Meatloaf. Ash was tall, long-haired, and fit for a bloke a year or two younger than me. The woman Ash had the hots for was a biker, leather waistcoat over a tight t-shirt, jeans, boots, and a mop of hair. She wasn't a classical beauty, but I could understand why Ash was attracted to her."

"You never heard her name mentioned," said Gus.

"Of course I did," said Paul. "Mandy, the girl who was murdered. I saw her again at the Winchester Gate the first Saturday we played with Down South. She was behind the bar."

"Down South was the band you started after Ash left," said Blessing.

"We played under the old name for a while. Several venues had posters out already, but punters and landlords associated Nimbus with Ash being on stage with us, and they were disappointed when only four of us arrived."

"Why choose the name Down South," said Gus.

"That's where we play," said Paul. "We don't travel further than a forty-mile radius of Winchester, so we gig in Wiltshire, Dorset, Hampshire, and Surrey. So they're all down south, get it?"

"Did Ash ever get lucky with Mandy?" asked Gus.

"Not that I noticed," said Paul.

"Someone did, though," said Gus.

"I told you. I don't mix with the women at our gigs. It wouldn't be good for my health. Did I see her leave one of the gigs with a guy? A handful of times, perhaps, but although he tried hard, Ash wasn't her type and got nowhere."

"Mandy met John Crees on the Monday night Ash stormed off," said Gus.

"I know that now," said Paul. "It was on TV and in the papers for weeks. They met at a gig, went out for several months, and then moved in together. Mandy worked at the Winchester, and her partner worked with a building firm if I remember right."

"Mandy worked at the Housing Department during the week," said Blessing.

"That's right, I remember reading that," said Paul. "The pubs where we played were the only places I ever set eyes on Mandy."

"You and your band members knew very little about Ash," said Gus. "Apart from the fact he owned a Vauxhall Combo van. Any chance you can remember the registration?"

Paul Price shook his head.

"Sorry, no. I can tell you he played a Gibson SG Special through a Marshall mini-stack, but I don't suppose that will help?"

"Hardly," said Gus.

"If he were such a good musician, surely another group would have snapped him up?" said Blessing.

"Down South has been doing the rounds of pubs and clubs in the region ever since that night, and we've not seen him or heard anyone mention him," said Paul.

"Unless he kept the nickname you gave him, that's unlikely," said Gus. "You insist Ash never gave much away about his past, but was there an occasion when he spoke about something that excited or annoyed him? You know, a comment unconnected to music."

Paul Price thought about what Gus had said.

"The only thing that comes to mind was when we visited Haslemere in Surrey. Ash arrived thirty minutes before we were due on stage, and there wasn't time to talk about it until the end of our first set. When I asked what made him late, he said he'd driven into town on the road from Liphook and stopped to view some new builds on a small development plot. So I asked whether he was looking to buy a place."

"What did he say?" asked Gus.

"Ash shook his head and said gigging with us gave him extra spending money, but he needed a big payday."

"What did you think that meant?" asked Gus.

"I thought it meant whatever he did for a daytime job barely covered his board and lodging and kept his van on the road. But, like many people, they need a lottery win to afford the new house they've got their heart set on."

"Can you pinpoint the date of that Haslemere gig?" asked Gus.

"A Saturday in the middle of August 2012," said Paul. "We played at a wedding reception in a huge marquee for crazy money."

"You need to get to your next industrial estate," said Gus. "Thanks for your help, We'll let you get on."

"I didn't think I helped at all," said Paul Price. "You must think we were stupid to stand on stage next to someone for so long and not know a thing about them."

"That's not for us to say," Mr Price," said Blessing. "You only knew what Ash was prepared to tell you. Which suggests he had something to hide, don't you think?"

"I suppose it does. But, hang on, do you think Ash killed Mandy and her partner, the guy who owned the Harley? She died because she turned Ash down, and the biker died because Mandy fell for him."

"We need to find your ex-guitarist to ask where he was on the night in question," said Gus. "What happens after that will depend on his answer. When you next meet up with the members of your band, could you ask whether anyone has a clue where we might start to look for Ash? Here's my card. Call me if someone remembers him mentioning a flat, a house, or a caravan."

Paul Price took the card.

"Will do, Mr Freeman. I'll get the mower onto the trailer and drive to the other side of Winchester. Two more sites to visit today, and then I'm taking tomorrow off."

Gus and Blessing returned to the Focus.

"Where to now, guv?" asked Blessing.

"Back to Sparsholt, I think. The Plough lunch menu looked passable, and the landlord was lighting the log fire as I left. So we don't need to rush back to the office, do we?"

"If DS Mercer wants to contact us, he would never think to ring the Plough at Sparsholt," said Blessing.

"That promotion to Detective Sergeant is in the bag, Blessing," said Gus.

"You seem happier, guv," said Blessing. "Although Paul

Price didn't think he'd been accommodating, I'm guessing we're closer to the finishing line than we were an hour ago."

"Almost there, Blessing," said Gus. "There's someone I need to speak to first. For that conversation, I need to go alone; it could be painful."

# Chapter Twelve

GUS DROVE them back to The Plough. They ate a hearty lunch, surrounded by villagers who weren't fazed by two unfamiliar faces. Next, Gus outlined his updated theory on the case. Blessing considered it for a while and gave Gus the thumbs up.

"We need to find Ash," she said. "Even if DCI Crocker gets the word out we've stopped investigating the double murder, DI Stanton and DS Baker could still be in danger because they're hunting Gillian Lye's killer. Ash might try to put a stop to that."

"Can you think of anyone else connected to John Crees and Mandy Howard we haven't spoken to?" asked Gus.

"No, guv," said Blessing. "Why have you?"

"Yes, but to get hold of him, I need to return to someone I spoke to earlier."

"Who might that be, guv?" asked Blessing.

Gus's phone rang. He looked to see who was calling.

"That's the trouble with mobile phones," said Gus. "In the old days, I could spend a quiet hour in a pub going over a case with my sergeant, and my superiors couldn't get hold of me."

Gus answered the call.

"Geoff. You've finished your meeting. I tried to get hold of you earlier."

Blessing watched as Gus listened to DS Mercer.

"Understood," said Gus.

"Do we have to get back to the office, guv?" asked Blessing.

"I'm on gardening leave until further notice," said Gus. "You will rejoin Grace and the Farm Watch people tomorrow morning."

"Was the PCC annoyed at you disrupting his speech?" asked Blessing.

"I don't think that helped," said Gus. "But ACC Mark Colbourne from London Road was on the Amesbury by-pass this morning, and he saw us in my car heading towards Winchester. Geoff Mercer hit the roof and reminded me I'd been ordered *not* to interfere in the ongoing investigation."

"Why didn't you tell him you knew who killed Gillian Lye?" asked Blessing.

"I think it's best we do what DS Mercer wants for now," said Gus. "I'll make sure he realises you were only following orders. I'll call an old acquaintance tomorrow and update you on any progress I make on Friday night at the Waggon & Horses."

"Won't you get into more trouble?" asked Blessing.

"What's the worst they can do," said Gus. "Sack me?"

Blessing looked at her watch.

"If we leave now, you'll reach the bungalow at the same time as Suzie. You need to tell her what's happened."

"I expect the gossip has spread around the London Road offices already," said Gus.

"DS Mercer will have contacted Amazing Grace," said Blessing. "After I've persuaded Jackie Ferris to let me have a snack this evening, I'll input today's events into my laptop. Then, I'll ask Grace if we can leave early tomorrow to drop the laptop at your bungalow. You can add your reports to the digital files. Don't worry about what happens next. Bring my laptop to the pub on Friday night, and I'll do the necessary. When we return to the Old Police Station office, our contribution to the Crees/Howard/Lye case will be synced in the Freeman files."

"Except for my conversations over an intervening couple of days," said Gus. "Right, let's get moving. There's nothing more we can do for the time being."

Gus drove to Worton Farm and dropped Blessing by the kitchen door. There was no sign yet of Grace's orange Smart car. Blessing was right. Gus had hardly set foot in the bungalow before Suzie came through the front door.

"What did I tell you, Gus Freeman? Don't put yourself, and your colleague, in danger. Keep away from Salisbury, and let the Bourne Hill detectives get on with their murder investigation. Now you've done it. Geoff had no choice but to suspend you."

"Finished, darling?" said Gus. "We didn't go anywhere near Salisbury, as it happens. Neither of us was in danger today. Geoff overreacted. No doubt, the PCC wasn't best pleased that I walked out of the office while he was recording a 'look-at-me' spot for Points West tonight. The only thing missing was that dreadful dog he was holding the last time he appeared."

"Where did you go then?" asked Suzie.

"Winchester," said Gus.

"Why?"

Gus told her everything Paul Price had told them and

suggested a trip to the Plough at Sparsholt for Sunday lunch would make a pleasant change. Suzie was both intrigued and annoyed.

"So you've already eaten and are prepared to ignore Geoff Mercer."

"I can multitask," said Gus. "Cooking us two different meals isn't a problem. As for tomorrow, I'm visiting someone I've known for years. So what's the harm in that?"

"I won't be able to persuade you to stay home," said Suzie. "Just be careful, Gus. If you're right about this Ash fellow, he's killed three people."

"It's Chris Stanton and Noah Baker you should be worried for, not me," said Gus. "They're on the case now."

"Can't you warn them?" asked Suzie.

"I dropped a few hints in Bob Mears's ear," said Gus. "Give him time, and he'll come up trumps. Enough about work; what can I get you to eat?"

### Wednesday, 5 December 2018

AMAZING GRACE ARRIVED outside at eight-twenty, and Blessing handed Gus her laptop.

"Where are you off to today, Blessing?" he asked.

"Bromham, guv," said Blessing. "That's part of the county I've never visited."

"Have a nice day," said Gus.

Suzie left for work at eight-thirty with another stern warning to Gus that he should leave things to the detective team from Bourne Hill.

Gus followed one set of orders by updating his files on Blessing's laptop with everything they'd learned yesterday.

When that task was completed, and he'd checked twice, he'd saved the file; he made a phone call. The lady of the house answered.

"Sally," said Gus. "Is Mike still home?"

"No, he made a miraculous recovery, as usual. He joined Mike junior on Monday morning to ensure their latest contract was on track. Did you want to speak to him?"

"Maybe later," said Gus. "I'd appreciate a chat with you first, Sally."

"I'm intrigued," said Sally. "Are you coming here?"

"I'll be forty-five minutes, give or take," said Gus.

"Coffee and biscuits will be ready," said Sally.

Gus ended the call and then rang a number at London Road.

"Divya Yadav, how may the Hub help you today?"

"Divya, it's Gus. Can you check on someone for me, please?"

"Of course, give me the details, and I'll call back when I'm done."

"Could you pass it to me on Friday night? You and Arjun will be there, won't you?"

"Intriguing," said Divya. "No problem, we're looking forward to a night out."

Gus thanked Divya and left the bungalow, and drove to Wessex Road.

When Gus parked the Focus on the driveway, Sally Woodman opened the front door.

"Come in out of the cold, Gus," she said. "Let's talk in the kitchen. It's warmer in there."

"Biscuits again, Sally," said Gus. "You're spoiling me."

"I can't think how I can help you," said Sally. "I couldn't add to what Mike told you."

"Tell me about Mike's business," said Gus. "You

mentioned retirement and the fact Mike keeps insisting he can't afford to stop work yet. After you moved here from Dorset, his firm's fortunes picked up substantially, didn't they? Mike told me he could take on more employees, bid for bigger contracts, and often got them too."

"We couldn't have done it without his half-brother," said Sally. "Tim invested money in the business. Sometimes, I wish Mike had never heard from him again. If he'd stuck to being a small concern, we would never have been million-aires, but we would have done okay."

"Tim Harding inherited money from his birth mother," said Gus. "His wealthy stepfather lived in Surbiton, and Tim's mother survived him. So when she died, a sizeable sum passed to her only child."

"Over four hundred thousand," said Sally. "Tim invested most of it in Mike's new firm."

"Tim wanted to be a silent partner," said Gus. "Silent partners get paid depending on their contribution and their equity in the business. Do you know what arrangement they had?"

"Mike told me they agreed Tim would get a share of any profits, but what percentage they decided on, I don't know. Before 2003, Mike was employed by a series of small firms. Only because of Tim's money could he contemplate going on his own. Mike did well almost immediately, and the improvement in his income allowed us to move here in 2006."

"Was there ever a downturn in business or profits?" asked Gus.

"Mike says the building trade is like a roller-coaster, and like a roller-coaster, it keeps going round and round and up and down. A peak always follows a trough."

"Mike told me last Friday that on Monday, the twenty-second of October 2012, he was due to drive to a spot near Old Sarum to start groundwork on a plot of land he'd bought for development. He said that day would be the first step towards five four-bedroomed luxury properties to strengthen his pension fund. So what happened to that development?"

"It fell through," said Sally. "People living in houses nearby objected, claiming there was a covenant on the stretch of land between their properties and the Country Park. It said that neighbouring owners should not cause annoyance. The houses in the crescent at the end of Hilltop Way didn't have the right to a view of the parkland, but they successfully argued in court that any new development between them and the parkland *would* cause annoyance. So, those five houses never got built."

"A development like that would have brought substantial profits, I presume?" said Gus.

"Mike thought so," said Sally. "Tim was annoyed Mike didn't know about the covenant."

"Hadn't Mike checked the land title was free of any caveats?" asked Gus.

"Mike wouldn't tell you this, but he has dyslexia," said Sally. "So, he asked John Crees to visit the Land Registry office in Salisbury in September when they were considering the purchase. John must have missed the significance of the covenant."

"Let me get the timing straight, Sally," said Gus. "When did this matter go to court?"

"About six months after John Crees and his girlfriend were murdered. You know how lawyers stretch everything out to justify their fees."

"When did Mike first learn there was a problem?" asked Gus.

"He had a letter in the post on Saturday morning, as did Tim," said Sally. "Typical of Mike, he looked at the legal language and put the letter to one side. Then, he would ask John whether it was anything to worry about on Monday."

"Then, on Monday, John wasn't waiting for a lift to work," said Gus. "Mike drove to the site, started work, and decided to check what happened to John when he got home. We know what happened when he reached Rampart Road. When did Mike next hear from Tim?"

"I can't remember," said Sally. "Mike was in a state for days. We all were. All work on the site stopped until he returned, and then the site closed pending the court case result."

"If Mike had understood that lawyer's letter, he would have realised their hopes of a big payday were dashed," said Gus.

"Things were tough for the next eighteen months," said Sally. "The firm was treading water, and profits were squeezed. Mike weathered the storm, but that abandoned development has been a big factor in him not having retired."

"What can you tell me about Tim Harding?" asked Gus. "Where does he live?"

"Do you know what they say about Chuck Norris?" laughed Sally.

"You don't find him; he finds you," said Gus.

"That's Tim, alright. He phones Mike from a public phone box to keep in touch, perhaps every three months. I've never seen him. He's always collected his mail from a post restante in Winchester because he claimed he didn't have a permanent address. He wasn't a traveller but wanted to stay off the grid. Mike sends him a cheque for his share of the quarterly profits and an audited set of accounts each year."

"Is he working, do you know?" asked Gus.

"We don't know," said Sally. "It can be tricky if he hasn't got a permanent address. Mike doesn't mention Tim that often, but when we have spoken about him, we thought with the remainder of the inheritance, plus his quarterly cheque, he wouldn't be living on the streets. Mike joked about it. He said he wouldn't be surprised to see a horse-drawn gipsy caravan outside this house one day, and Tim would knock on the door."

"So, you don't know what he's done with his life since he and Mike left school?" said Gus.

"I don't," said Sally. "I didn't need to know. Tim is Mike's half-brother and has never attempted to get close to our family. He wanted somewhere to invest his money, and Mike accepted when Tim got in touch out of the blue because Tim was family in his eyes. Nobody else ever offered to help Mike start his own business. Tim could be a successful entrepreneur or a hippie. We'd be none the wiser."

Gus told Sally everything they had learned since reopening the case.

"I can't believe it," said Sally. "You must have it wrong, surely?"

"I've passed the search to a colleague in Devizes," said Gus. "She's got his birth details and will hunt for an address in Surbiton when he was a teenager. The man we're searching for was driving a Vauxhall Combo in 2011, so there's a chance his driving licence has a photograph. We'll check whether he's ever applied for a passport. His accent was described as part London, part Californian. Maybe he's travelled to the States and worked there. When I meet my colleague on Friday night, I expect to find that Tim Harding and the guitarist formerly known as Ash are the same person."

"I ought to phone Mike," said Sally. "The news will shatter him."

"I'm sorry for being the bringer of bad news," said Gus. "When you sit down with Mike and go through the sequence of events, there can be no other explanation. Mike and Tim received news about the covenant from the lawyers on the same day. Tim realised his dreams were over. In one of those quarterly phone calls, Mike probably told Tim that John Crees was intelligent and taking on more responsibility. Mike could leave business matters to John where his dyslexia proved problematic. Tim already knew John and Mandy lived together. The lawyer's letter was the last straw. John Crees had stolen the woman he loved, and now he'd robbed him of his big payday. That's why they both died that night and why their deaths were so violent."

Sally followed Gus to the front door.

" I'm sorry, Sally," said Gus.

"Don't be," she said. "You were only doing your job. Tess was right. You're never beaten as long as you have one more thread to follow."

Gus drove back to the bungalow—time to update the Freeman files.

# Epilogue

ON WEDNESDAY EVENING, Gus and Suzie dined at the Lamb with Clemency and Brett. The main topic of conversation was the wedding, and while Brett discussed the reception with the landlord, Gus sat quietly, reviewing the past week's events. Beside him, Suzie and the Reverend chatted and made notes.

They walked along the lane together at closing time and agreed to meet again on Saturday evening for another trip to the Fox & Hounds.

On Thursday morning, Gus made Suzie breakfast, waved her off to work at eight-thirty, and started the list of chores she'd provided. Then, as he sat down for a well-earned coffee break in the middle of the afternoon, his mobile phone rang.

"Afternoon, Gus. It's Bob Mears here. We heard the news, mate. I hope they'll see sense soon. Nobody will call you to put you in the picture, but Catherine Gumm didn't find anything different from her original assessment when she did the autopsy this morning. Phil Crocker just confirmed that Gillian Lye was strangled. The killer wore gloves and didn't leave any fibres or DNA traces."

"I expected nothing less," said Gus. "Anything else?"

"Stanton and Baker have just left the office on their way to Merthyr Tydfil. Mandy Howard had a two-year affair with a guy called Eifion Edmunds. He was married, and she wanted him to leave his wife, but he wouldn't, so she ended it. Not a scenario to make Edmunds chase across the country to kill Mandy and her new lover. Phil Crocker still wanted them to check the guy out, just in case."

"The answer lies closer to home, Bob," said Gus. "If I wasn't on gardening leave, maybe I could help."

"You certainly started something with that bug hunt," said Bob. "Phil's got us checking under every pot plant to ensure nobody's listening in. I think he's losing it."

Gus thanked Bob for the information and ended the call —time to finish hoovering the bedrooms.

### Friday, 7 December 2018

SUZIE BREEZED through the door at five-thirty. Gus was in the lounge reading the local paper.

"Are you ready?" she asked.

"We're not due at the Waggon & Horses until nine," said Gus.

"I want to do the weekly shop tonight like we did last week. Then, we'll grab something to eat on our way home."

"While we drive to the supermarket, will you tell me about your day?" asked Gus. "Time drags when you're at home, alone."

"You've only got yourself to blame," said Suzie.

"I have a feeling tonight will be a watershed moment," said Gus. "Those dark clouds will part, if only for a moment."

"What have you been up to now?" sighed Suzie.

Three hours later, they had stored away the shopping, eaten a chicken curry, and were in Suzie's Golf heading for Harrington End. When they reached the Waggon & Horses, Suzie spotted several familiar cars parked on the side of the road.

"I think we're the last to arrive," she said.

She parked on the grass verge, and they entered the back bar. The team were already there, plus Divya and her husband. Neil Davis was centre stage.

"Just in time, guv," said Neil. "I've put money behind the bar, get yourselves a drink, and I'll tell you our news."

"Terrific," said Gus. He ordered a pint and a soft drink and leaned against the bar with Suzie as Neil told his tale.

"On Tuesday, we arrived at the hospital at four in the afternoon. Melody was put on a monitor, and routine checks were carried out. Her waters had been leaking since Monday morning, and she was stressing about the possibility of infection. The doctor and a midwife had various conversations over the next two hours, and they decided it was best for Melody to be induced. At half-past eight, another midwife who came on shift at six applied some gel, and Melody remained on the monitor for an hour. She was getting mild contractions, like the ones she'd had for the past few days. At midnight they gave her a second dose of the gel. The doctor told us not to worry. Melody would be in labour before morning. Her waters finally broke at half-past two. The contractions suddenly became a lot stronger. Half an hour later, she was on the gas and air. At this point, Melody did a complete U-turn on her objection to having an epidural. She reckoned the pain was horrendous. As the sun rose, the nice midwife was back on shift and encouraged Melody to start pushing. They didn't seem to be getting anywhere. Melody was getting more emotional by the minute, eager to be done with it all and desperate to see our baby. Everything was quiet, so I popped out for a coffee. I was only gone for three or four minutes. When I got back, it was action stations. The baby's head had been born. The midwife checked the cord wasn't around her neck. Another two pushes, and out she came, screaming. Beatrice weighed in at three and a half kilos, or seven pounds eleven ounces in old money. Melody never even needed a stitch."

"Beatrice, what a lovely name," said Lydia.

"When did you get the pair of them home, Neil?" asked Alex.

"Yesterday evening," said Neil.

Lydia, Suzie, and Divya kept Neil occupied for the next ten minutes, allowing Gus to speak to Blessing. He took her outside to the Golf, grabbed the laptop from under the front seat, and she stowed it in her oversized handbag.

"Thanks, guv," said Blessing. "Will it make good bedtime reading later?"

"It starts as a mystery, but I don't think it is anymore," said Gus.

They returned to the bar and were joined by Amazing Grace. She told him the Farm Watch scheme was gathering pace as more farmers signed up. Thefts in the countryside were rising steeply, and Grace thought home security systems, doorbell cameras, and CCTV in the towns and cities were driving thieves to softer targets. Gus told her to keep up the excellent work, and with luck they'd be working together again in the New Year.

Jamie was chatting to Arjun about cricket, which gave Divya an excuse to come over to speak to Gus.

"Let's find a quiet spot," said Gus. "Are you ready for another glass of white wine?"

Divya nodded. They moved further down the bar, and Gus attracted the attention of one of the bar staff.

"Spill the beans," said Gus.

"Tim Harding was born in Guildford in 1962. He left school at eighteen with top grades in three A-levels. His main interest was music. He'd played the guitar since he was fourteen, and the band he was with turned professional early in 1981. They toured in the UK and Europe, and although they enjoyed chart success in Sweden and Italy, their style didn't match the current trend in this country. Tim left in 1985 to join another UK band flying to the States to try their luck on the other side of the pond. The next time Tim's name cropped up in this country was in 1991. His musical career had stalled, and his physical and mental health was destroyed. Five years travelling from coast to coast, playing up to two hundred and fifty gigs each year had taken its toll."

"Drugs?" asked Gus.

"It seems most likely," said Divya. "However, he didn't fall foul of the law at any stage. He stayed with his mother and stepfather in Surbiton when he returned to this country. Then, in 1993, he started work."

"Surprise me," said Gus.

"Mercury Telecommunications," said Divya. "He stayed with them until 1997 when they merged with Cable & Wireless. After that, he went into business for himself, installing home and office security in the Thames Valley region. However, details on that are sketchy. He continued to give the family home in Surbiton as his permanent address, but neighbours don't recall seeing him in the area after 1997."

"Driving licence?" asked Gus.

"Passed his test before he went on the road with the first group. The DVLA say his licence is due for renewal in 2020. The photograph on his current licence will be key. Yes, he had long hair in 2010 or whenever he had that photo taken. It won't take a second for someone from Salisbury to confirm whether Tim Harding was the man who played the guitar in pubs and clubs back in 2012."

"So, Tim could have drifted around Buckinghamshire, Berkshire, and Oxfordshire for six years," said Gus. "What sort of footprint does he have on social media?"

"Not a scrap, Gus," said Divya. "Wikipedia has a page detailing the hit-and-miss careers of the bands he played with, but nothing about Tim Harding after 1991. He slipped under the radar from 1997, and I couldn't find anything concrete until late 2002 when his mother died. Solicitors handling her estate put a notice in the national press and regional newspapers. Harding must have seen they wanted him to get in touch and learned he'd been left everything."

"If he was scratching a living and found himself with the best part of half a million quid, why didn't he resurface and live the life of Riley?" asked Gus.

"Perhaps we'll never know," said Divya.

"I intend to make sure someone asks him," said Gus. "Have you traced his whereabouts since 2003?"

"His centre of operations moved from Thames Valley nearer the south coast," said Divya.

"Hampshire, and Surrey, with occasional forays into Wiltshire and Dorset," said Gus. "That makes sense. Paul Price met him in Andover, they gigged within easy distance for Tim to reach in an hour or so, and since 2003, he's used Winchester Post Office for his mail. What about that Vauxhall Combo? If only we had a registration."

"The Hub has access to similar departments with other forces," said Divya. "I've learned that an eleven-year-old Combo was spotted leaving the M3 near Winchester last Wednesday at three twenty-eight in the afternoon."

"Where was it heading?" asked Gus.

"Towards Winnall on the A33, but The Hub doesn't do half a job, Gus. A few miles further is a village called Kings Worthy, which has several caravan sites nearby. I have the details on my phone. Shall I send them to you?"

"I will be forever in your debt, Divya," said Gus.

"What are you going to do, Gus?" she asked, grabbing his arm. "Blessing told everyone the news when we got here."

"I intend to enjoy this evening and spend a quiet weekend driving around the countryside near Winchester with Suzie. Then on Monday morning, I'll drop into Bourne Hill Police Station to hand a package into Reception. My old mate Bob Martin can do the honours."

"Very mysterious, as always," said Divya. "Let's rejoin the others."

Alex and Lydia were next to collar Gus.

"How long will DS Mercer keep you from the office, guv?" asked Alex.

"I haven't spoken to him, Alex," said Gus. "Things to do, you know how it is. How's the early-intervention game going?"

"It has its moments, guv," said Alex.

"I've got a piece of news, guv," said Lydia. "Morris Beard phoned Raj Sengupta today and asked if one of his team, Rosie Allison, could come to see me next week. Any ideas?"

"There's no harm in listening to what she has to say, Lydia," said Gus.

When last orders were called, and Neil's taxi was waiting outside, the team said their goodbyes, and soon Gus and Suzie were alone.

"What terrific news for Neil and Melody after their earlier troubles," said Suzie. "Everyone seemed in good spirits tonight. Perhaps it's because Christmas is just around the corner. So let's get you home."

They walked outside the pub as a dark cloud obscured the moon.

Suzie grabbed Gus's arm as he stumbled in the sudden darkness.

On Monday morning, Gus was confident he could present DI Stanton and DS Baker with the tools to finish the job. In addition, he and Suzie had a wedding to attend in just over two weeks. As for the New Year and beyond, who knew?

## Next in The Freeman Files series

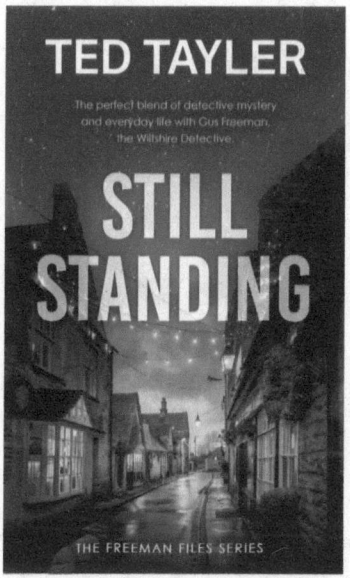

vinci-books.com/stillstanding

**A chilling conspiracy. A detective's final case.**

As DS Mercer's retirement approaches, a sinister discovery
emerges: a series of murders spanning back to 1998, all connected
along the M4. Could the killer be one of their own? Mercer
recruits Gus Freeman and the Crime Review Team to investigate
covertly, uncovering a shocking truth.

Turn the page for a free preview…

# Still Standing: Chapter One

**Monday, 10 December 2018**

"Do you think you'll hear anything from Geoff Mercer today about when you'll get back to work, darling?" asked Suzie.

"That rather depends on who's pulling the strings," said Gus.

"Surely, Kenneth still has the final say? He doesn't hand over the reins until the end of March. The name of his replacement hasn't even officially been announced."

"Don't worry about me. I'll be okay," said Gus. "Just eat your breakfast, sweetheart, or you'll be late."

"I'll keep my eyes and ears open at London Road if you wish," said Suzie.

Gus could tell Suzie wasn't going to let it go.

"A quick chat with Vera might prove beneficial," he suggested. "Nothing much goes on between the four walls of HQ without her knowing."

"Do you think Vera knows you're off to Bourne Hill this morning?" asked Suzie.

"If she does, there will be roadblocks at either end of the lane," said Gus.

"Don't joke," said Suzie. "If someone was watching us at the weekend, we'll both be for the high jump."

Gus drained his coffee mug and collected their empty plates. If he was to be on the road to Salisbury within the hour, he had to get a move on. So Suzie went to the bedroom to finish getting ready for work while he loaded the dishwasher.

When Suzie reappeared in her uniform, with her hair pinned, Gus joined her in the hallway.

"Have a nice day," he said.

"Just be careful," said Suzie. "I'll see you at the usual time tonight. Love you."

Gus nodded, and they kissed.

"Do you want me to walk you to the car?" he asked.

"Will you make a habit of it?" asked Suzie.

"Probably not," said Gus.

Suzie kissed him on the cheek, scooped up her car keys from the hall table and closed the front door behind her as she left.

As Gus got himself ready for the day ahead, he reflected on the hectic weekend they had just shared. Something he'd heard in one of his first conversations about the Rampart Road murders had refused to go away. It was ever thus. In his early days as a DC in Salisbury, his sergeant shook his head when Gus told him he had an inkling.

"Follow the tried and trusted method, young Freeman," he'd say. "It's there for a reason."

"I feel I'm right, sarge," Gus said, "even though I don't *know* that I am."

When Gus's intuition proved invaluable in solving a case, his sergeant put it down to beginner's luck. Nevertheless, they joked about it several years later when Gus had earned his three stripes.

"Either you're the luckiest copper that ever lived, young Freeman," said his sergeant at his retirement party, "or perhaps you'll turn out to be one of the best."

Gus hadn't realised the significance of his most recent niggle until last Wednesday morning when he visited Sally Woodman at her home in Wessex Road. After their conversation, everything fell into place. But because he was on gardening leave, Gus couldn't share his new knowledge with many people.

Suzie didn't get the full story until they'd driven across the border into Hampshire on Saturday afternoon, and Divya Yadav hadn't had any context to attach to the search requests Gus had asked her to carry out.

Bob Mears had called on Thursday to tell Gus the two detectives who had assumed full responsibility for the Crees and Howard case were following a false trail to South Wales. The news cheered Gus, as it meant they were out from under his feet. Finally, he could check he had the final pieces of the jigsaw without incurring the wrath of their boss, Phil Crocker. One more complaining phone call from Phil to London Road would be curtains.

Gus would have loved to have the rest of his team with him, but even before Geoff Mercer ordered him to stay home, his colleagues were scattered across the county. Amazing Grace and Blessing were ankle-deep in turnips near Bromham. Poor Lydia had to suffer long days at

Gablecross, listening to Raj Sengupta wittering on about the value of statistics.

At least Alex Hardy had been doing something worthwhile in Swindon last week, assisting the early-intervention teams. But Gus knew Alex was worthy of so much more, as was Neil Davis. So on Friday, when they all met up in the Waggon & Horses for a much-needed social night, they celebrated the arrival of Neil and Melody's bouncing baby daughter, Beatrice. Neil would be on paternity leave now, while the other team members were due to stay away from the Old Police Station office until the Christmas break.

As Gus had hoped, Divya had found the final missing pieces for his jigsaw, and the surfeit of good news meant he was drunk when the team left the pub. He'd spent Saturday morning recovering. By the time he and Suzie had returned to the bungalow in the early evening, they had discovered Tim Harding's address.

Suzie had first driven them to Winchester, where they paid a brief visit to the Post Office. Gus knew there was zero chance they would learn anything specific from staff due to the usual privacy restraints, but Suzie had a plan. Divya had done her best to enhance the image from Harding's driving licence, and Suzie used her charms on the young man behind the counter.

Resistance was futile. The young man agreed it *did* look like the guy who collected the post that arrived for him, although his hair was shorter. Gus asked whether they were expecting Mr Harding to call in anytime soon.

"I couldn't swear to when we last saw him, sir," said the youngster. "The whole point of setting up a poste restante is because you don't want people to know your permanent address, or you don't have one for a short period. So all I will say is that that man has been a regular visitor over the past eighteen months I've worked here."

"Would it be too much to ask whether he receives a lot of mail?" asked Suzie.

"How much would *you* receive if you subtracted the junk mail?" asked the young man.

"I take your point," said Suzie. "So, a handful of items on each occasion; is that fair?"

The young clerk nodded, then looked over his shoulder to see if anyone was listening.

"A few official-looking envelopes, a music magazine, and the occasional small package which needed a signature. That's about it."

Gus and Suzie thanked him and returned to the Golf.

"Divya confirmed Tim Harding has no social media activity," said Gus, "and we know he liked to be paid in cash wherever possible. I wonder whether he avoids the internet altogether?"

"Lucky chap, if he does," said Suzie. "Where to next?"

"Divya pointed me towards King's Worthy," said Gus. "Follow the High Street to Easton Lane, and that will take us to Winnall in ten minutes. But, first, we want the A34 out of Winnall, and then we look for caravans."

Divya's information was correct; there were several caravan sites to check. After cruising around two sites with no sign of a Vauxhall Combo van, Gus wondered whether they would be out of luck. However, he needn't have worried. As Suzie drove them slowly past yet another neat row of caravans on the third site, he spotted the van dead ahead.

"Okay, keep going at the same speed, Suzie," said Gus. "We're not stopping for a chat. They're all even numbers on this side, so Harding lives at number twenty-eight."

"Don't worry, I haven't looked directly at the caravan," said Suzie. "In case Harding is watching, I'll cover every inch of roadway to convince him we're prospective buyers rather than someone interested in him."

"When we get home, I'll spend half an hour putting the finishing touches to the case," said Gus. "Then we can enjoy the rest of the weekend."

After completing the circuit of the caravan site, Suzie eased the Golf into mid-afternoon traffic on the A34 and returned to Winchester. Gus kept an eye on the wing mirror for any sign they were being followed. He saw nothing to cause undue alarm, and sixty minutes after leaving Winchester, Suzie swung the Golf through the gateway at the bungalow. As she parked next to the Focus, her dashboard clock showed five-fifteen.

"Good timing," she said as they stepped into the hallway. "Could you work in the kitchen until six o'clock? Meanwhile, I will put my feet up in the lounge and watch TV. I need my rest before another busy evening."

"Of course, darling," said Gus. "What time are we meeting Brett and Clemency?"

"Trust you not to be listening on Wednesday night," said Suzie. "We're picking them up at seven-thirty. Our table at the Fox & Hounds is booked for eight."

"In that case, I think it's high time I drove," said Gus. "You've done more than your fair share at the wheel today. Since I over-indulged last night, I'll be the designated driver. We need to take the Focus tonight, anyway."

"Brett will feel guilty," said Suzie.

"He's getting married in little over a fortnight. So he needs to take every opportunity for a pint while he can."

Suzie dropped her car keys on the hall table and disappeared into the lounge. Gus fetched his file folder from the bedroom and made himself comfortable at the kitchen table. As the clock on the wall reached six, he was already reading through his final contributions.

The file should be sufficient for DI Stanton and DS Baker to bring the Rampart Road murders to a close after six years. But, of course, DCI Crocker wouldn't be happy, and his old pal, Bob Martin, would have a few words to say. He might suggest Gus wasn't handing Bourne Hill detectives a present, but instead, he was lighting the blue touchpaper and withdrawing before the firework exploded.

Gus returned the file to the bedside drawer and joined Suzie in the lounge. The TV sound was muted, and she was asleep, with her hands clasped on her bump. Gus let her rest and headed for the shower. As he dried himself, he heard a knock at the bathroom door.

"I've got the coffee on," said Suzie. "I must have nodded off."

Gus joined her in the kitchen five minutes later.

"Everything okay?" he asked.

"Tired, that's all," said Suzie. "Nothing to worry about. The little one was active while I was resting my eyes earlier."

"I didn't listen to Neil's every word about the birth on Friday night," said Gus. "March will be on us before we know it, and things will never be the same, no matter what Sylvia Robbins has up her sleeve."

"I didn't hear anything from Neil to frighten us," said Suzie. "Okay, Beatrice kept Melody hanging around for several days after her due date, but this one will arrive when ready. Every check-up I've had so far has shown there's nothing to worry about."

"I do hope so," said Gus.

Suzie knew Gus was concerned that with several guaranteed negatives in the first quarter of 2019, things might continue in the same vein regarding their child.

They drank their coffee in silence, and then Suzie went to get ready. They left the bungalow a few minutes after seven, and Gus drove them to the Rectory.

"The Reverend peeked through the curtains," said Suzie. "They know we're here."

"She's being sensible," said Gus. "No point standing outside on a night like this."

One minute later, Brett and Clemency hurried down the path and got into the back of the Focus.

"How are you both?" asked Suzie.

"Cold and hungry," said Clemency.

Gus drove to Nursteed Road and parked in the Fox & Hounds car park. With Christmas around the corner, plenty of people were already inside, and hopes of a quiet chat were out of the question.

Clem and Suzie went to find their table while Gus and Brett waited, in turn, to get served.

"Any news, Brett?" asked Gus.

"I wish there were something positive to tell you, Gus," he said. "Bert's causing Irene a few concerns. She told us this afternoon that he's called her Cora on more than one occasion."

"I never met his wife," said Gus. "Bert told me they'd been married for fifty years when she died in 2005."

"Irene reckons Bert's become more confused since that bout of flu," said Brett.

"I suppose sharing a house with someone different after you've been alone for thirteen years, could be enough reason for a slip of the tongue."

"Fair comment, Gus," said Brett. "But Irene said Bert has stopped leaving the house for his regular constitutional to the allotment and the Lamb. Instead, he spends hours just sitting in his chair."

"Not unusual for someone his age, Brett," said Gus.

"A couple of times this week, Irene said she spoke to him, and Bert didn't seem to hear. Irene thought he'd nodded off, but when she repeated the question, it was as if he didn't know where he was for a while before answering."

"Did Irene call a doctor?" asked Gus.

"Bert told her not to bother," said Brett. "You know what he's like with the medical profession."

"I do," said Gus. "He avoided visiting the Lamb for years when he knew the local GP would be in the bar, holding court over a gin and tonic."

"Bert's view is if he made regular visits to the surgery, that would be the finish of him. They'd start him on tablets for symptoms he'd managed himself for decades, and kick-start ailments he'd never suffered before."

"Bert believes in traditional methods of healing," said Gus. "Hard work and a regular dose of cider. What does Clemency think?"

"Clem's seen similar symptoms among her parishioners," sighed Brett. "It's generally a sign the brain is shutting down, one tiny bit at a time. They don't have a major stroke but a succession of episodes where they drift off in the manner Irene described. So we're even more convinced we made the right choice in bringing the date forward for the wedding. We can only hope we still have time, I'm afraid."

A member of the bar staff finally caught their eye, and they ordered their drinks. Brett didn't comment when Gus ordered a slimline tonic. When they edged through the crowded bar, Gus spotted Suzie and the Reverend deep in conversation.

"Sorry we took so long," said Brett. "This place is busy tonight, isn't it?"

"Did you girls get a chance to study the menus?" asked Gus.

"We've ordered," said Suzie. "Clem could see you two chatting at the other end of the bar, so we grabbed the opportunity when the landlord stood idle. With the Christmas menu in force since the first of the month, there's less choice than usual."

"Brett would have ordered steak if he'd been here," said Clemency. "So, I took an executive decision."

"So did I," said Suzie. "You're having what he's having."

"I can't argue with that," said Gus. "It's far too early for a Christmas dinner."

Although he enjoyed his succulent steak, plus all the trimmings, Gus was more concerned with Brett's news about Bert. Gus made a mental note to visit his old friend after he returned from Bourne Hill.

For the first time in ages, the girls didn't want a dessert, so while Brett chatted to Gus about the latest animals to come through his office door, Clemency brought Suzie up to speed with the wedding preparations. Finally, just before closing, they threaded their way through the crowds to the front door and into the car park.

Gus drove them back to Urchfont and dropped Brett and the Reverend at the Rectory.

"Will we see you on Wednesday?" asked Suzie.

"I'll call you if there's a problem," said Brett. "I promise."

Gus and Suzie had made the short trip to the bungalow and were in bed before eleven, which made a welcome change from the previous night. In the morning, Gus had made their breakfast, or rather brunch.

"I'm going to drop in to see Bert and Irene tomorrow morning after I've dropped the file into Bourne Hill," said Gus. "Perhaps, I can persuade the old buzzard to see a doctor."

"Good luck with that," said Suzie. "Have you seen the weather out there? It's decidedly cold, wet, and windy, so we'd be wise to stay indoors and keep warm."

Gus couldn't argue, so they listened to the wind buffeting the bungalow walls and the sleet rattling against the window panes for thirty minutes. Then, they took turns selecting a vinyl album.

"I wonder what genre of music our little one will prefer?" asked Suzie.

"Their education has already begun, perhaps?" said Gus. "Are you getting any feedback? Lots of kicks during Fleetwood Mac to suggest dancing, or no activity to indicate disinterest when your middle-of-the-road selection is playing."

"Experts say you should play classical music, or lullabies, to soothe them," said Suzie. "What our child just made of Sister Rosetta Tharp; I can't imagine."

Gus had leafed through his albums for an early Bob Dylan. Suzie agreed it was quieter and more soothing than his earlier choice, but they had argued whether it was a classic until bedtime.

Gus smiled at the weekends' memories, grabbed his coat and scarf, and carried the folder to the car. The wind was still gusting, but the sleety rain had stopped during the night. He eyed the dark clouds scudding across the treetops and shivered—roll on the spring and warmer temperatures.

A watery sun was breaking through the clouds when he arrived in Salisbury. Gus parked in the visitors' car park at Bourne Hill and looked north. The blue-black sky suggested there was a storm brewing twenty-five miles away. Hard to tell from this distance, but Gus could almost hear Kassie Trotter moaning that the shortest day wasn't due until Friday week.

Gus walked into Reception with fingers crossed. He was in luck, Bob Martin on duty.

"I wasn't sure we'd see you again, Gus," he said. "That lanyard I issued you with won't get you very far, I'm afraid. You've been cancelled."

"I come bearing gifts, Bob," said Gus. "I don't doubt Phil Crocker was on the blower to you when he heard from Geoff Mercer. Bob Mears called me on Thursday evening, which shows not everyone here considers me persona non grata, despite my being on gardening leave. Have you seen Stanton and Baker this morning?"

"They're back from the valleys," said Bob. "A complete waste of time was how they described it. I couldn't fathom why they spent four days there, but Cardiff played Southampton on Saturday afternoon. I reckon they had a few beers in the city centre in the evening, and whoever was driving couldn't risk it until the afternoon."

"I'm guessing that was football," said Gus. "Look, could you see Dumb and Dummer get this folder, please? There are no long words, and it's self-explanatory."

"Have you done their job for them, despite being told not to?" asked Bob.

"I was ninety-nine percent of the way there before I received the instruction to stop, Bob," said Gus. "It seemed churlish not to complete the task. Tell them I'd be thrilled for them to take full credit. With luck, that will stop them from dropping me in it."

"I'll do my best, Gus," said Bob. "Don't worry. I won't breathe a word to Phil Crocker."

"Thanks, Bob. I'd better make tracks," said Gus. "Look after yourself."

"You too, Gus. Oh, before you disappear into the sunset, I heard good news at the weekend. Maxine Devereux has agreed to return to work full-time."

"Now that *is* something to put a spring in my step," said Gus. "Maxine and her husband live out at Winterslow, on the border with Hampshire. I visited her a few months back during the Kendal Guthrie enquiry and was introduced to her son, Oliver. He'll be seven months old now. I doubted whether we would ever see Maxine at Bourne Hill again; she seemed content. Why would anyone swap that life for the greasy pole?"

"Rumour has it Maxine is returning as a Detective Inspector," said Bob. "The salary increase might have persuaded her to tear herself away from little Oliver. However, her husband's situation probably impacted her decision more."

"His name was Gary, wasn't it?" said Gus. "I'm afraid I don't follow the sports pages as assiduously as Neil Davis, one of my sergeants. Has Maxine's husband lost his place in the team?"

"Gary suffered an injury a month into the new season, and although it wasn't career-ending, the club has younger players who can play in his position. So, no doubt, they'll be keen as mustard to cement their place in the first team while he's out of action. You know what young guns are like. Gary's forecasted to get back to full fitness by the end of the season, but, likely, he'll only be guaranteed second-team appearances next season. So, the Devereux family will feel the pinch."

"I don't suppose I'll get to see Maxine at work," laughed Gus. "Who do you think will be the lucky DS to work with her?"

"I don't know too many people from Dorchester HQ out at Winfrith," said Bob. "That's where I've heard she's heading."

"Our loss is Dorset's gain," sighed Gus. "Why is it every piece of good news has a 'but' attached lately?"

The phone on the desk in front of Bob rang, and he shrugged.

"No rest for the wicked, Gus," he said with a wry smile.

Gus left the building and returned to the Focus. His work here was done, and to heck with the consequences. As he drove across the Plain towards the tenebrous skies he'd observed earlier Gus hoped he could find a bright light somewhere in his day.

An hour later, with noon fast approaching, he drew up outside Bert Penman's home. He walked up the path to the front door, glancing at the front garden as he went. There was never much to brighten the mood in mid-December. Everyone's garden was dormant.

Gus remembered Bert and Irene had worked together in the autumn, tending the shrubs and deciduous trees. Whether they'd had the energy to tackle the orchard at the rear of the property was another matter. Gus made a mental note to ask Brett if he'd helped his grandfather keep things in order this year. His old friend wouldn't want his place to become as untidy and unloved as a few others in the village. Bert was a stickler for standards—fat chance of finding an old pram or discarded sofa in his garden.

Irene North answered the door when Gus rang the bell.

"Mr Freeman," she said. "What brings you here?"

"I feel guilty, Irene," said Gus. "My visit is long overdue. Suzie and I haven't seen the pair of you in the Lamb for weeks. Brett told us the flu jab had come with an unwelcome bonus."

"I should say," said Irene. "Come into the kitchen. It's too cold to stand on the doorstep."

As Gus followed Irene into the kitchen, he heard the radio in the next room.

"Coffee?" asked Irene.

"Black, without," said Gus. "Bring me up to date, Irene."

"I kept clear of coughs and colds for years, but the surgery kept badgering me about needing extra protection this winter. They had the cheek to say we were vulnerable. Bertie wanted to tell them where to stick their needle, but I finally talked him around. I thought it would be more beneficial for him, being that much older than me. I only went with him to make sure he didn't back out. Within a week, we were in bed: separate beds, Mr Freeman. So you can drop that raised eyebrow. That bout of flu knocked us both sideways, so it did."

"Brett told us," said Gus. "You seem more like your old self now, Irene."

"Cheeky," said Irene. "I've never been short of a word, Mr Freeman. My late husband, Frank, would have confirmed that. But as the years have flown by, talking is the only thing I can still do at the same pace as when I was a young woman. But, no, it's not me; Bertie is causing us the greater concern."

"Is he sat in his chair next door?" asked Gus.

"That's about all he does these days," said Irene. "He might be awake if you'd like to go in. I'll bring your drink through in a tick. I made Bertie a cuppa not thirty minutes before you arrived, and we don't tend to have lunch until half-past one. He won't mind hanging on for a while."

Gus left Irene pottering in the kitchen and opened the front room door. Bert was staring out of the front window, perhaps listening to the voice of a female presenter. The time signal on the hour confirmed Bert was tuned to Wiltshire Radio and a topical conversation.

"Hello there, Bert," said Gus stepping into the room.

Bert turned his head slowly. Then, when he recognised his visitor, he scolded:

"You should be at work, Mr Freeman. Gus, I mean."

Gus took a chair from the table in the centre of the room and sat beside his old friend.

"I know you'll find this hard to believe, Bert," said Gus. "But I've been a naughty boy. My bosses have put me on gardening leave with no definite date for me to return."

"They must want their heads read," said Bert. "Turn off that radio, will you? Cora switched it on when she brought me a drink. I'd rather have her company than that silly woman prattling on about the economy."

Just then, Irene came in with Gus's black coffee. He got up to switch off the radio.

"Many thanks, Irene," said Gus.

"He does that a lot, Mr Freeman," whispered Irene. "I don't mind. We're good friends, that's all, but Bertie never used to get my name wrong before he had that blessed flu."

Irene returned to the kitchen. Gus didn't stop her. He could tell she didn't want Bert to see she was upset.

"Brett tells me you haven't been to the Lamb lately, Bert," said Gus. "Nor the allotment, although not much needs to be done this side of Christmas. I've spent less time there myself due to the cases we were looking into before I got my marching orders. Do you think you'll feel up to visiting the allotment soon? My time's my own for the foreseeable, so I can drive you whenever you say. If you spot something that needs urgent attention, I can deal with it, under your guidance, of course. Afterwards, we could drop in the pub for a pint."

"I haven't felt like walking to the Lamb. It's been cold and wet," said Bert. "I've got a couple of flagons of cider in the house if I want it, but apart from a whisky, or a brandy, to warm me, I haven't bothered."

"I could tell the two of you tidied the front garden before you were taken ill," said Gus. "Irene must be a comfort?"

"She does her best," said Bert, "but she's not my Cora. We didn't get around to the greenhouses and the trees at the back, though. Brett reckons I should phone for a tree surgeon to see to my orchard in future. What's the point of me if I haven't got something to keep me going? I never thought it would come to this. I'm tired, Mr Freeman, ready to go on."

"Do you remember when I moved here, Bert?" asked Gus. "I hardly knew one end of a rake from the other, and the Four Seasons were a bunch of lads from Newark, New Jersey. After Tess died, I spent days sitting outside my garden shed, asking why me. You coaxed me back from the precipice with a few words here and there. The hours we've spent together have been some of the best of my life."

"It was my pleasure, Mr Freeman," said Bert. "You weren't like the others, like Frank North. You listened. How long is it you've been in the village now?"

"A little over four years," said Gus.

"Then it's too soon to say you'll make a good gardener," said Bert, "but you're on the right track."

"I need you around to keep me on the right track, Bert," said Gus. "I'm not the only one. Brett and Clemency need your guidance too. Married life can be tricky, and you and Cora had fifty years together. You raised two children, and you can pass on the wisdom you learned from that experience if, and when, the time comes."

"Is Miss Ferris, Suzie, keeping well?" asked Bert.

"She's fine, Bert," said Gus. "You'll be able to raise a glass to our little bundle before spring has had a chance to settle in."

Bert chuckled and gazed out of the window.

"That would be good, Mr Freeman," he said.

"Call me when you're ready, Bert," said Gus. "You and Irene enjoy the rest of your day."

# Still Standing: Chapter Two

Gus took his empty cup back to Irene in the kitchen.

"He's not right, is he?" she said.

"Bert's eighty-six, Irene, and none of us can expect to be in perfect health at that age. So I've told him I can be available during the day to give him a lift anywhere he wants to go."

"Perhaps I can get Bertie interested in going out, Mr Freeman. He might snap out of his melancholy if we all do our bit without pressuring him. I overheard you telling Bertie you weren't working at present. Do you ever regret coming out of retirement?"

"Heavens, no," said Gus. "I've made new friends, kept my brain active solving a few mysteries, and I would never have met Suzie if I'd spent the rest of my days feeling sorry for myself."

"There's an upside to everything, isn't there? Well, thank you for calling, Mr Freeman," said Irene. "It means a lot. I'm sure it means a lot to Bertie, too. He thinks highly of you."

"The feeling's mutual, Irene," said Gus. "Even if I suddenly get a frantic call from the Chief Constable saying they can't cope without me, I won't be a stranger. I'll pop along the lane to see you both as often as possible. I promise."

Irene walked with Gus to the front door. When Gus sat in the car, he looked back. Irene was wiping a tear from her eye as she closed the door.

Gus drove slowly along the lane to the bungalow, swung the Focus through the gateway, and parked under the rambling roses. As he stepped into the hallway, he thought a bowl of soup was called for. Twenty-five minutes later, thanks to his store of fresh vegetables and his invaluable soup maker, he had a bowl full of goodness, plus a doorstep hunk of bread from the end of a wholemeal loaf. It wouldn't make everything right in the world, but it helped.

After tidying the kitchen and checking whether Suzie had left a list of chores he'd overlooked, Gus sat in the lounge. He noticed the vinyl albums they'd listened to had been put back in a rather haphazard fashion. Nine months ago, that would have annoyed him.

Times had changed, and anyway, with Suzie's eclectic taste added to the mix, there was little point in applying logic to how they were stored. So Gus made another mental note, not to mention that to her.

Gus was daydreaming when the phone rang in the hallway. He came back to the present with a start. Could it be the lady who once asked for Dorothy? Was she back again after so many months?

"The Freeman residence," said Gus.

"Behave yourself, Gus," said Vera. "Kenneth wants a word."

"Oops," said Gus. "I thought I had a day or two's grace, at least."

"I've no idea what that's supposed to mean," said Vera. "I'll put him through."

Gus held the phone away from his ear, just in case.

"Freeman, are you there?"

"Yes, sir," said Gus. "How may I help?"

"You can't," said the Chief Constable. "I just want you to listen. The PCC has been in touch concerning Ms Logan Barre."

Gus suddenly recalled a brief conversation he'd had with Lydia on Friday night.

What was it she'd said? Morris Beard had made a courtesy call to Raj Sengupta, informing him his colleague, Rosie Allison, would visit Lydia at Gablecross this week to chat.

Blimey, they were quick off the mark. Gus had already had a few drinks that night and perhaps unwisely told Lydia there was no problem listening to what Rosie had to say. Was that a schoolboy error?

"Freeman, are you still there?"

"Of course, sir," said Gus. "I was waiting for the punchline."

"Their initial conversation was concluded this morning," said Kenneth. "Ms Logan Barre is going to the Old Police Station office tomorrow morning to meet the other team members."

"Good idea, sir," said Gus. "It never pays to be too hasty, though. Was there anything else?"

"I doubt you'll be happy to hear this, but the official announcement regarding my replacement will be made on Friday. ACC Robbins will face the Wiltshire press corps for the first time on the steps outside this building."

"Best tell her to wrap up warm, sir," said Gus. "If the weather isn't frosty, the reception from the media will more than make up for it."

"You sound remarkably cheerful considering your present circumstances, Freeman," said the Chief Constable. "I can't help thinking you've pulled a fast one. Something I've yet to hear about."

"If there's nothing else, I must go, sir," said Gus. "I thought I heard the postman outside."

Gus rang off before Kenneth could grill him further, went to the lounge, and turned on the TV. After watching two antique dealers on a road trip in Wales for an hour, he realised he was dreading the next two weeks. He needed another case to solve.

Suzie arrived home at five-thirty to find Gus hard at work in the kitchen.

"Something smells delicious," she said. "I'm not complaining, but this *is* Monday."

"I was bored," said Gus.

" How was Bourne Hill?" asked Suzie.

"I only stayed long enough to deliver the case folder. Then Bob Martin told me Maxine Devereux was ending her maternity leave and moving to Dorset, which wasn't welcome news."

"That's a shame," said Suzie. "You hoped to persuade Kenneth that Maxine would be the perfect fit for the Crime Review Team."

"That was weeks ago," said Gus. "When I still hoped the team would stay together regardless of whether I was there."

"You've heard the announcement about ACC Robbins' appointment then?" said Suzie.

"Kenneth rang this afternoon," said Gus. "Not about her Friday meet-and-greet with the press. I fear the PCC's team are already trying to poach Lydia. Kenneth told me Rosie Allison spoke to Lydia this morning, and tomorrow your friend Sarah will continue the PR campaign in our office."

"You knew Lydia was bound to move on at some point, Gus," said Suzie. "Kenneth warned you not to rely on her being in the office throughout the coming months. He wanted Geoff Mercer to send her to different departments to show Lydia what was available. Sooner or later, your rising star will decide which path she wants to follow. I'm going to shower and change. How long before dinner?"

"Fifteen minutes," said Gus.

After they'd eaten, they sat in the lounge with a coffee, and Gus told Suzie about his visit to Bert and Irene. She sympathised with Irene's lot and agreed they must drop in whenever they could over the coming weeks to offer what support they could.

"We need to be subtle," she said. "Not something you're good at, darling. Bert will dig his heels in and refuse to budge if he thinks we're interfering. Perhaps I can persuade the Reverend to involve Irene in the wedding preparations. That will keep Irene busy, and with odd reminders lying about the front room, Bert will realise he does have something to look forward to."

"That's a good idea," said Gus. "It could be beneficial for me, too. Can you put together a list of things you'd like done between now and Christmas? Anything to keep me from daytime television."

Suzie lay her head on Gus's shoulder.

"Poor you," she said.

**Grab your copy...**
**vinci-books.com/stillstanding**